BENEATH THE POPPY FIELDS

Christopher Chance

To: Tom
with
Best Wishes

Christopher Chance

Strand Fiction

First published 2020 by Strand Publishing UK Ltd
Registered in England & Wales Company Number 07034246
Registered address: 11 St Michael Street,
Malton, North Yorkshire, YO17 7LJ

info@strandpublishing.co.uk
www.strandpublishing.co.uk

Paperback edition

ISBN 978-1-907340-25-3

This book is dedicated to my lovely wife Susan

At the going down of the sun

And in the morning

We will remember them

Foreword
by
Mark Wingett

A year or so ago I watched the documentary "They Shall Not Grow Old" by Peter Jackson. He had taken the jerky, contemporary, black and white and sometimes damaged film footage of the First World War and told the story of trench warfare in the early 20th Century Fields of France. Using the recorded eyewitness accounts of survivors as commentary, he upgraded the film stock into modern colour high definition footage. It is a remarkable achievement that for a want of better words leaves the viewer shell-shocked and moved to tears.

Chris Chance achieves the same here with this superlative novel. Based on real characters and true events we follow the adventures of Widnes Colliery Foreman Johnny Gordon and his fellow colliery miners as they "sign up" as Sapper (Royal Engineers) and are taken from their families of Northern England and thrust in the "Satan's Abattoir" of Northern France.

With only three days military training, Sergeant Johnny and his gang are brought in to combat their German counterparts who have been destroying British positions from below the battlefields, excavating tunnels and laying mines.

In this particular Hell of Mud, we get to know Johnny and his band of tough, heroic, subterranean warriors.

Chris as ever writes from the heart. The men speak in their Northern dialects. The language is uncompromising and shot through with a dark gallows humour as they perform their grim duties, often at the behest of their naïve, dangerous, vainglorious upper class officers. Death can come in an instant, yet they persevere.

It is a privilege to be in the company of Jonny, Solly, Taff and the band. And their wives too, who back home find their own particular way of comforting themselves.

It's a remarkable, visceral novel. It shows the best and worst of mankind. I salute these brave men as I can almost smell the cordite and feel the cold stinking battlefield mud of Northern France, like death clinging to me. Such is the power of Chris's writing…

I sithee Johnny, I sithee…

Lest We Forget

Mark Wingett
2nd November 2020

CHAPTER ONE

The warm September breeze moved the corn in slow waves across the farmers' fields, as high in the clear blue sky the skylarks chirped their quirky songs, but not in the same fervour as when they had young to sing about, for the broods had long since hatched and flown the nests. In the distant fields farmers were busy harvesting the last of their crops.

Away in the distance to the north could be seen the smoke of St Helens, to the east lay Burtonwood and Warrington, to the south the chemical town of Widnes belched its stinking fumes, and due west was open country all the way to Liverpool about twelve miles away across the farmers' fields beneath which lay the rich coal seams of Lancashire about two thousand feet down.

Late summertime in England was truly delightful just then, especially for Johnny Gordon, as he gently kissed his beautiful wife Jane, whom he calls Jinny. They were having a picnic and lying together on their picnic blanket, having just eaten one of Jinny's tasty pork pies, fresh out of the oven that morning. The remnants of the picnic occupied the furthest corner of the blanket, except for two bottles of black stout nestled in the shade at the edge of the cornfield. Leaning on his elbow looking down into her lovely brown eyes his hard face softened as his deep blue eyes took in the beauty of his young wife.

"One day we'll have kids," he whispered.

"Not 'til we have our own house," she replied, "I'll not have kids while living with my mother and our Billy in t' house. Bloody oaf he is."

"Billy is a miner, just like me. He works like a beaver at t' coal face and…"

Jinny pushed him, got up on one elbow and glared at him.

"And he behaves like one when he comes up out t' pit. He's a bloody animal."

Johnny leant over to grab a bottle of stout, yanked out the cork and glugged it practically in one, leaving just an inch in the bottom of the bottle. He held it out.

"Here, 'ave a swig o' t' ale, goes well wi' t' pie."

"We isn't low bred tha knows, so stop acting like our Billy, an' get me t' other bottle. His behaviour is rubbin' off on thee so mebbe it's time t' flit[1]."

Johnny finished the bottle and leant back to grab the other. Pulled the cork out and wiped the top with his sleeve and handed it over. Jinny demurely accepted it and took a sip as ladylike as she could and passed it back. This little act was another reason Johnny loved her so much and she knew it. They collapsed, laughing and kissing on the picnic blanket. Johnny looked down into her eyes for a serious moment and whispered.

"We can't flit. Ma needs our rent money and times'll get harder wi' this war 'n all."

"There's a house comin' empty in Kent Street an' I want it. Ma can come wi' us, but not Billy; he can stay where he is. His girlfriend will move in wi' him when we flit."

"Thee's a crafty lass, Jinny. I bet thee knows when we're flitting. I bet thee's got it all worked out."

"Come on, let's go home; thee's on t' night shift tonight," said Jinny.

"Aw, an 'ere's me thinking about a kiss an' cuddle in t' sunshine before…"

She fairly flew at him, landing right on top of him giggling and kissing as he fell back off his elbows to lie flat on his back as she straddled him and pulled up her skirts so she could feel his manhood rapidly grow, poking into her inner thigh.

"Tha' must have seen up my skirts, didn't ye?" Jinny said.

"Why?" Johnny smirked.

---

[1] flit – to move house

"I forgot to put my drawers on this morning an' ye must have seen my thatch."

Johnny watched her face as she gave him a moue, a blown kiss, like a pout, which to Johnny was the signal to penetrate. He hunched up and unbuckled his leather belt and pushed his trousers down, allowing his full-blown erection to brush against the thick bush of soft hair.

Johnny knew what was coming next. She teased the glans by controlling the sliding motion along her clitoris as Johnny felt her wetness and then she allowed only the glans to enter. Johnny tolerated her notional power over him because he knew this was her paradise and would only last another moment before she swallowed him wholly into her innards where she would transcend into the most intense orgasmic joy. It was not long before Johnny spurted his seed into her and there they lay, entwined, kissing and stroking each other.

"Tha's being naughty," Johnny said.

"I can't help it. I want to go again," Jinny said, as she again squeezed those special magic muscles only women have, "an' ye may as well come in me again, cos right now I don't care an' I felt ye coming in me, it wuz warm an' splendid, an' now I can feel ye growing inside me an' I want to feel it again, warm an' splendid."

The warm sun shone on the lovers as they continued nature's beautiful ritual, which inevitably concluded with sighs and kisses, the insects and skylarks being the only witnesses.

Johnny grabbed the picnic blanket and flapped it clean of crumbs as Jinny stood to flick her long, billowing, ankle length skirt and pat it back into shape. She did not need Edwardian style corsets to show her curves, just a tug on the ribbon that acted as a belt to display the tiniest of waists. She tucked in her linen shirt and displayed her pert breasts before hiding them behind a baggy waistcoat. Far from being a twentieth century lady of fashion, Jinny was working class and proud of it, her man was a foreman collier at the coal face and she was a skilled seamstress and dressmaker.

Johnny picked up the empty beer bottles and popped them into the picnic bag with the remaining debris. Only a flattened patch of grass was evidence of their presence here, as they strolled away from their beauty spot along a cart track winding between hedgerows toward home.

Home was a row of terraced cottages badly in need of refurbishment, especially the slate roof tiles of which many were broken. Scruffy boys played with spokeless bicycle wheels they called trundles or hoops; girls skipped and sang as they jumped a long rope stretched right across the street. The noise was loud and happy but tomorrow they would be quiet because their fathers were working the night shift tonight so they would play somewhere else.

Johnny pushed open the front door and stepped back to allow Jinny into the house. He stepped in behind her to see his mother-in-law placing lumps of coal on the fire. The fire was in the centre of a large cast iron range with ovens on either side and a large black kettle hung above the fire on a hook fixed somewhere up the chimney. There were copper pans on top of each of the ovens quietly bubbling away in the heat of the late summer, but this was their traditional way of cooking and coal was free to miners so the home was warm summer and winter.

"Leave that, Ma. I'll do that," said Johnny as he winked at Jinny and nodded at the teapot. "Jinny'll make a brew an' we can all have a read afore we eat."

Ma stood back arching her back with her hands clasping her lower back as she looked at the ceiling.

"Bloody coal scuttle's getting heavier and seems further away from t' coal-hole in t' yard. Ain't doin' my bloody back any favours, our Johnny. Mebbe get one wi' wheels on."

"Good idea Ma. Yer brain's wasted 'ere. I bet there ain't a coal scuttle in t' world wi' wheels on."

"Don't thee take t' piss, our Johnny. Jinny's father'd kick your arse all aroun' t' yard if that feckin' coal hadn't fell on 'im. God rest 'is soul."

4

"I'm not jokin' Ma. It's a good idea an' some bugger'll be rich one day when the idea becomes reality, you wait an' see."

Jinny was preparing the dining table and laying it for tea. There was only one table in the house so it was used for all kinds of things including Jinny's dressmaking, so she cleared all her paraphernalia and her brother Billy's unfinished jigsaw puzzle. She carefully placed everything on the sideboard and looked up to see the picture of her father hanging just a few inches above her, his stern face with its thick moustache and bushy eyebrows glowering at her.

"That's one arse thee'd never be able to kick; ye crusty old bastard," she whispered.

Johnny sat on one of the four sturdy wooden chairs surrounding the dining table and opened a newspaper.

"Where's Billy?" he asked. "He better not be down t' pub."

"Said he was goin' t' Widnes," said Ma, "then goin' t' Clock Face village t' see his girlfriend. He'll be home for teatime. He knows what's on t' stove."

Jinny noticed the concerned expression on Johnny's face as he read the newspaper.

"What's up?" she asked.

"Bloody Germans are killing thousands of our men in t' war and they said it'd be all over by Christmas and that was last bloody year," replied Johnny, as his eyes met hers over the top of the newspaper.

She could not quite conquer that now familiar chill of fear as they realised the war crept ever nearer to home and the chances of separation grew daily.

"Mebbe ye should stop readin' t' bloody newspapers, they're bloody evil and full of blithering shite," said Jinny, as she pulled out a tray from the oven.

A large freshly baked loaf of bread sent a tantalising smell wafting through the house.

"Just in time," cried Billy as he stepped through the front door, "I nearly broke into a trot when I got a whiff o' that down t' street."

The war was forgotten as Johnny's rowdy brother-in-law dragged a chair, noisily scraping it across the flagged floor.

"Cut us a chunk o' that loaf, our Jinny. I'm drownin' in saliva just now, the smell is drivin' me mad."

"Yer already bloody mad and thee can wait 'til we all sit down to eat. Yer manners are gettin' worse since thee's been seein' that tart in Clock Face village."

Billy gave an exaggerated sigh and a sulk Michelangelo would love to have painted. He was a handsome lad, big for a seventeen-year-old, with curly blond hair and a hard body, sculpted over the last three years at the coalface. He was happy and carefree and appeared unconcerned that his life below ground would be shorter than that of the men working the fields in the fresh Lancashire air.

"Sithee[2] our Johnny; that posh bugger, the officer, Hellfire Jack, is on t' way up 'ere from London to get miners an' Manchester tunnellers t' join t' army. They reckons he's even takin' t' grave diggers and…"

"Bollocks, who the hell is they?"

"Ring o' Bells landlord's brother has a pub in London an' knows all about it."

"That's bloody ripe," said Johnny. "So, all t' Kaiser's generals'll know by now cos Flanders is nearer to London than we are."

Talk about the increasing threat of war put the wind up Jinny. She slammed down the hot baking tray and marched through the back door on her way to the lavatory across the yard, kicking chickens out of her path as she went.

"Now look what thee's done,' said Johnny. "Wi' all that shite about t' war, she's gone t' privy just as we're about to eat. Y' know how nervous yer sister is lately. Bloody think afore ye opens cakehole."

Feeling guilty Billy went to the back door and called across the yard.

"I'm sorry, our Jinny. Come on back in t' house. I won't say nowt about t' war again, honest."

---

[2] sithee – see you/ know this

6

In the waning light of early evening the privy looked like a sinister little house, much too big for what it was used for, hence the term built like a brick shit house. Behind the closed wooden door of the privy, Jinny had put the lid down on the toilet seat and sat on it, pulling her skirts around her legs - she hated the spiders that lived in there. Of course, with the door closed making it dark, she was not going to be long thinking about the consequences of war. She noticed that the newspaper, cut into squares and hung on a nail in the wall, needed replenishing. Toilet paper had not yet reached the shopping list of miners, or any working class homes in 1915. She reached up and pulled the chain, thereby noisily flushing the toilet, letting them know she was about to return and get on with the evening meal, which incidentally is called tea in this corner of England.

She swished her skirts to rid herself of imaginary spiders and smoothed the outer skirt down over her petticoats as the noisy cast iron water cistern refilled, after discharging more than a gallon of water through the down pipe into the lavatory bowl. She stood in the doorway looking at the evening sky wondering what was to become of her if her man went to war. The caw-caw of a passing crow jolted her so she quickly went indoors and was greeted by Billy's loud voice.

"Food for the Gods is what we get, our Jinny," boomed Billy. "Yon lamb's kidneys are makin' my mouth water, an' the bread. I hope my wife can cook like ye 'an Ma?"

"What bloody wife?' asked Jinny. "Yon Clock Face tart is not marrying thee while I'm alive. I've heard she's flattened more grass around here than farmer Kelly's Friesians."

"Whoa," said Johnny, "we're about to eat and tempers are rising so let's nip this in t' bud." Looking at Billy he told him, "Thee's too young fer marriage so forget it," turning to Jinny, he said in a calmer voice, "Please don't rise t' bait every time Billy tries it on. Tha knows he's takin' t' piss. Now let's all sit down to our lovely tea. We're workin' nights this week and grub like this makes it all worth it."

That night at eight pm Johnny and his men entered the cage of No 3 Shaft at Bold Colliery and were lowered to a depth of one thousand eight hundred and fifty one feet where they worked a twelve-hour shift before returning to the surface. A miner's life was hard and dangerous and often short lived, hence the strong bond of comradeship between tough, hard men of the north. Nevertheless, Johnny was a strict disciplinarian and his fists were the tools of his trade. That did not help Jimmy Golden, a long time member of Johnny's crew, when a large stone weighing about two tons dislodged and crushed him to death near the coalface during the final night shift of the week. Trade Union rules and Health and Safety guidelines were in the far distant future during the summer of 1915.

Jinny entered the bedroom at three pm on the dot, with a steaming cup of tea as ordered by Johnny when he arrived home from the colliery that morning. She placed the cup on the bedside cabinet and silently opened the curtains allowing bright sunlight to light up the room, as she sat on the edge of the bed looking lovingly at her man. There was a tiny shard of coal embedded into his cheek just beneath his eye, which had not been washed out during the early morning shower before leaving the colliery. Actually it was not a shower but a hosepipe running cold water onto a brick floor, which Johnny often used instead of using the galvanised iron bath at home like most of the other miners did. She picked at the shard of coal with her fingernail and a trickle of blood emerged from the punctured skin as it came out. She quickly licked it clean then stuck a thumbnail size piece of newspaper on the tiny wound and watched as the red blood blossomed outwards like a rose before the bleeding ceased. Johnny's eyelids fluttered momentarily and a moment later she was gazing into the blue eyes she loved so much.

"I've brought your tea, Johnny, and your newspaper."

"Thanks, Jinny, thee's a diamond, giz a kiss!"

He grabbed and pulled her on top of him as she giggled happily in their private moment, but the caress ended abruptly as he remembered Jimmy Golden.

"Sorry, Jinny. I've got to get over to Sutton to pay my respects to Jimmy Golden's family."

"I know," she said, "I'll make us a picnic for when thee gets back and we'll go t' Owl's wood and call in t' pub on t' way home."

"Aye, lass. That's a grand idea. No wonder I love thee so much, giz another kiss!"

That was one kiss too many as she snaked her tongue into his mouth and reached beneath the sheets to grab his manhood, which responded instantly. She thrilled inwardly when he whispered hoarsely into her ear.

"Ma is downstairs so ye must move slowly wi' out shakin' t' bed, take tha drawers off an' climb on."

"My drawers are already off, but I want to see it afore ye puts it in."

She deftly straddled him in the 69 position and teased him with her tongue. He responded by teasing her with his. Ma did not hear any bed shaking because they both exploded into orgasm together without penetration.

The early morning sun saw men wearing clogs and miner's helmets, noisily marching along the lane towards the coalmine. This was the morning shift, which relieved the night shift at eight am. They would work until they were relieved at eight pm by the night shift. Shifts changed weekly so these men would work nights the following week.

Weaklings did not last long down a coal mine because of the strength and guts required to be part of the team that attacks the coalface and gets coal to the surface. These men were all muscular, sinuous athletes in the unsporting world of subterranean digging where danger lurked in many guises and claimed many lives; a breed of men from generations of the same families - digging in the same coalmines where fathers, brothers and sons who had fought the coalface for decades.

Johnny's brother-in-law, Billy, larked about with a big strapping man called, Solly, a Liverpudlian, and Taff, a wiry Welshman. The jolly pushing and shoving caused annoyance as others got jostled amongst the banterers. Johnny called a halt to the jostling as they approached the colliery gates where a shiny Rolls Royce motor car was parked and a group of men in suits stood next to it, all looking concerned and terribly serious. One man stood out from the gathering as he stepped up and onto the running board of the car. Dressed immaculately in tailored Royal Engineers uniform he addressed the men with his impressive patrician accent and strong baritone voice.

"I am Major John Norton-Griffiths of the Royal Engineers and I am here to recruit men to join brave men digging under the German lines in France. Your country needs you now more than ever, not in the trenches, but beneath them, setting charges that blow the Bosch to hell where they belong. You will be paid higher wages than our normal soldiers and more than you earn here at the coal face."

The miners looked on in awe at the man they already knew about through reading newspapers, and here he was, Hellfire Jack, as he was more commonly known amongst the mining community - a millionaire engineer and Member of Parliament for the Conservative Government no less. However, like all British soldiers he referred to the Germans as the Bosch, the Hun, Fritz or Jerry. Some of the men shuffled away to start their shift but Johnny remained, looking at the recruiting sergeant with his sheets of paper and pen at the ready, using the Rolls Royce bonnet as his recruiting desk.

"Sign up here," shouted Hellfire Jack, as he stood up taller on the running board and uttered his favourite line, "kill the Bosch now so your wives and children never see their bayonets coming for them down your street. Conscripted men will not be paid as much as volunteers and conscription is coming very soon. Think about that!"

Billy was first in the queue to sign the grinning sergeant's sheet of paper, who then handed him a new kitbag.

"Nine o'clock train in t' mornin' at Widnes Central station. Yers'll be in Chatham barracks tomorrow night. Thy pay starts today, Sapper," said the sergeant.

"Sapper," asked Billy, "what's that?"

"Thy rank as a private soldier in t' Royal Engineers, Sapper William Nolan," said the grinning sergeant. "Get used to it and thee'll have a number by tomorrow night."

The sergeant playfully ruffled Billy's mop of golden blond hair.

"An' thee can say tarra to thy goldilocks tomorrow, barbers an' t' baths tomorrow night."

Sheepishly Billy looked to Johnny, deciding whether or not to put his helmet back on and start his shift or to march up the lane back home. Johnny looked on, face steel cut, as his day shift team disintegrated before his very eyes and joined the army. He was torn between love of England, his wife and his sense of duty. He also realised he could not dig coal on his own alone at the coalface. The word conscription sprang to mind so he needed to decide. The very thought of joining the army to go to war created a chasm of stress in his chest which he felt was immediately filled by an anvil. He very nearly threw up. Never before had he experienced such traumatic inner turmoil in the making of a decision.

"Sithee, there's two of us to consider in our house so wait 'til I come back. I'm off home."

Everyone watched him march back along the lane.

"He'll be back," said Billy.

In the terraced row of two up, two down miners' houses, Jinny, arms folded, was talking to neighbours when the lady next door pointed up the lane and stuttered.

"Bloody hell, somet's 'appened at t' pit. Your Johnny's comin' down t' lane."

Johnny's natural gait made him look somehow menacing and sinister. He did not march or take long strides but ambled along with bunched fists as though he was going to hit something when he got there - out of earshot some men called him Iron Arse. The sight of the approaching Johnny sent a chill wind of concern through the

11

group of miners' wives. Jinny broke away and walked fast towards him as the others dispersed to spread the news that something was not quite right at the colliery. Johnny's hard face frightened Jinny.

"What's 'appened?" she cried.

"The army is at t' pit recruitin' t' lads. They're all signing on. Your Billy was first in t' queue. He's a soldier now in t' Royal Engineers. That posh bloke, Hellfire Jack, is there. Tha' knows, the one as always in t' paper."

"So wharrabout thee?" Jinny asked.

"I can't go down t' pit on my own so I've come home to tell thee about it."

Her eyes widened with the decision she had to make. Her face was stricken with uncertainty. He reached for her as she collapsed sobbing into his chest. His heart broke as he whispered in her ear.

"Duty calls, my dearest sweetheart. We knew this day would come, but listen, we are working underground, not on t' battlefield an' we get higher wages than down t' pit."

"Have ye signed on?"

"Not yet, that's why I've come home, so we can talk about it."

She stiffened and held him at arm's length, glaring at him with big watery eyes that melted his soul.

"Your love of country is not as strong as your love of me, else you would have signed on. Go now and sign on. I'll put t' kettle on an' make a fry up so don't be long."

There was a cheer when Johnny came marching back to the colliery. Hellfire Jack recognised leadership quality when he saw it and whispered to his sergeant.

"Put him down for three stripes. Jerry is in for a surprise."

After signing on the dotted line the sergeant handed Johnny a paper travel warrant with all the men's names on.

"Thee's in charge t' travel arrangements and bah gum thee'll make sure each man arrives at Chatham Barracks at teatime tomorrow."

"I'm not responsible for this lot,' said Johnny, "I'm t' boss down t' pit, not out 'ere in t' street."

"Thee's in charge now. Acting, unpaid Sergeant Gordon."

"Acting, unpaid. What in fuck's name does that mean? I do fuck all unpaid," said Johnny, as he bunched his fists ready to start punching. The sergeant very nearly soiled himself as Johnny's ice blue eyes and granite face loomed closer.

"Stop there!" the authoritarian voice of Hellfire Jack cut through the tension and stopped Johnny in his tracks.

"You will be paid as a sapper until the end of the month when your probation ends and you earn the substantive rank of sergeant. Until then, you are Acting Sergeant Gordon."

Momentarily puzzled, Johnny nodded approval and looked at the list of names on the travel warrant. In his gravelly voice, reserved for telling people off, he called out the men's names.

"Billy Nolan, Peter Salisbury (Solly), Gareth Dupree (Taff), Robert Alcock (Allballs), Andrew Emans (Andy), Thomas McKinney (Kinney), Colin Howell (Brummie), Thomas Tudor (Tat) and Barry Bliss (Yiggs). All in t' Griffin t' night wi' wives or girlfriends."

Billy looked blank and moaned.

"We 'aven't been paid. I 'aven't any money fo t' pub."

Hellfire Jack stepped forward and harrumphed loudly.

"The colliery management will take care of that right now."

Hellfire Jack glared at the suited gentlemen as though he was about to shoot them. That worked. Having decided nobody else was signing on at this colliery Hellfire Jack and his sergeant drove off to the next colliery on the itinerary, as Johnny strolled out of the gates counting his money followed by all the men in his team of coalface miners. Apart from Jinny, all of the miners' wives and girlfriends were in for a hell of a shock as the men headed home to impart the news.

Brummie's wife, Ruth, opened the bedroom curtains allowing the bright sunshine to enlighten the task of changing the bed linen. After laying a fresh sheet and pillowcases she looked through the bedroom window to see the big, strapping, young, Albert Jennings loitering on the street corner awaiting her signal. She opened the bedroom window and shook the small bedside rug outside, which was the all clear signal for Albert Jennings to approach, making sure no neighbours were about to see his entry into Brummie's house.

She watched him stroll along the street, all six feet four inches of muscular youth with a handsome face and curly blond hair, which excited her to the core, soaking her underwear as she envisioned his penetration of her desirable body, which she knew was irresistible to young Albert, whose impulse was to ejaculate the moment his glans slid into her, which is why she knew that first dynamic burst would be down her throat. This was the forbidden fruit, the fresh passion, the immense gorging of young Albert's vibrant shaft, which stoked the fires in her belly. The thoughts of it sent her giddy as she heard his footsteps on the stairs.

His handsome head appeared first, apprehensive but smiling with desire as she slowly let her skirt fall to the floor followed by a tug of her drawers as she wriggled them down past her knees to kick them off completely onto the skirt on which she stood fully erect, showing off her bright ginger bush. The apprehension in Albert dissipated instantly with the wondrous vision before him, the bright sunlight illuminating the colour of her hair, driving his manhood forward like a telescope just opened in his trousers. Ruth could not help herself as her desire drove her forward to pull off Albert's braces and pull down his trousers, which placed her head right there, facing the object of her wanton lust. Without a word she took the head of his shaft into her mouth, which immediately exploded with a gush of semen as Albert's sensations shook the wax in his ears. Moments later they were on the bed with Albert exploding again inside her as she moaned in ecstasy with her own explosion of orgasm and the demanding of more of the same.

Ruth was truly surprised as she heard the clatter of clogs approaching their terraced house. Over the years she had come to recognise Brummie's footfalls. The realisation it was him approaching their front door created a kaleidoscope of challenges she thought she could not win. So she panicked and threw young Albert Jennings off her naked body when the clatter ceased outside her front door, which was never locked. Brummie opened the door and stepped inside their snug living room and called out.

"Are ye in, Ruth, I've got some news for thee?"

Upstairs there was a numbing silence, then panic as Ruth tried to shove young Albert under the bed. There was a dull clang and a splash as his head hit the chamber pot, splashing stale, stinking urine down his face and into his mouth. A splutter escaped his throat as he gagged on the vinegary taste and his eyes smarted with the acid contents of Brummie's and Ruth's bladders. The realisation that Brummie, the miner with the most frightening reputation of bone-crushing fights, had arrived home to find young Albert, naked in his bedroom with his also naked wife, was enough to churn his innards to liquid mush and the impelling urge to vacate his bowels.

"Just coming, darling," Ruth shouted. "Put t' kettle on, I'll be down in a minute."

Brummie sat in his favourite chair and started to take off his clogs as Ruth whispered to young Albert.

"Don't move until I get him out of the house then get dressed and fuck off."

"I'm shitting myself," Albert cried, "I can't hold it any longer."

That was the moment when gasses and solids flew out of his arse, so loud even Brummie heard it.

"Are ye all right up there, Ruth?" Brummie asked.

"Just coming, dear,' Ruth said and as calm as she could as she quickly dressed and whispered to young Albert, "Ye clean that up afore ye goes."

"I think we'd best go out. If I stunk like that, I'd go t' doctors," Brummie said, as he laced up his shoes. "C'mon, let's go t' doctors, ye ain't well. I'll empty t' po[3] when we gets back."

Ruth grabbed her coat and bag and scurried out through the door leaving young Albert to dispose of any compromising evidence.

---

[3] po - chamber pot

15

In the street outside Johnny's house Ma had hold of Billy Nolan and was beating him around the ears, hurting herself more than Billy.

"Ye gormless feckin' git, why'd ye join th' feckin' army?" Ma said.

"Cos I'll get more than if I was conscripted. Leave off, Ma!" Billy snapped.

"More what? Feckin' brains is what thee needs more of," Ma said.

She gave him a last clout across his face and a sharp knee into his bollocks, sending him to the ground clutching himself in the ghastly pain of testicle trauma.

"That's what thee'll get more of where thee's going," Ma said, her heart breaking with the prospect of her only son going to war, "you feckin' idiot."

The noise and laughter in the Griffin pub was music to the landlord's ears as he pulled pints of frothing ale for the men and beer shandies for the women. An old bloke started thumping the old piano and the singsong was soon roaring out of the pub's windows frightening the birds.

"This is the night to remember," said Johnny, "laughter and singing and on t' way home, the night birds, and the rustling and smells of the countryside will stay with me until I come back."

Jinny snaked her arm around his hard waist and looked up into his sparkling blue eyes, bright in the darkness of his face, his peaked cap shading his good looks from the lights of the pub. As handsome as he was she could see something about him that others might say was sinister which made her think of the old adage *still waters run deep*.

"Sithee, be thyself an' take no risks an' thee'll come home all right. Don't look out for our Billy or any t' others, they're all tough men and nays why they signed on," Jinny said.

"Mebbe thee sees things better 'n me but there's a bond down t' pit that cannot be broke," Johnny said.

"You ain't down t' bloody pit," she snapped. "Yers 're goin' in bloody trenches an' 'oles in t' bloody ground where there ain't no coal."

He lifted his pint and savoured the taste.

"Bloody ale down south is flat 'n cloudy so I'll have another t' remember t' taste."

"Get me one," she said, "so I can remember t' taste too. I won't be comin' in t' Griffin 'til thee comes 'ome."

"Aye, lass, comin' up," he caught the landlord's eye. "Two pints please, landlord."

The pub was full of men going to war, some of them from other shifts and some from other departments of the colliery. Johnny's men gravitated around him and Jinny as the landlord called last orders. Solly raised his pint glass and roared a toast.

"Here's to a short war and a safe homecoming!"

A great roar of approval and cheers erupted in the pub, shaking the timbers and the patriotism could be cut with a butter knife. The only glum face was that of Yiggs Bliss; he was miles away in thought. Taff nudged him.

"Penny for 'em?"

"I am so happy knowing I'm not goin' down t' pit ever again an' I'll be breathin' the clean fresh air of France and gettin' away from this fuckin' awful shitty hole in the ground," Yiggs replied.

Billy Nolan laughed.

"I'll fuckin' drink to that an' what about those French lasses? I'll have some o' that," he cried.

Jinny caught his eye.

"Broadening thy horizons, are ye? Just make sure ye don't bring no frog tart back here. You're supposed t' be seeing a girl in Clock Face."

"Aye, will ye tell her where I've gone when she comes lookin' for me?"

The night ended with everyone traipsing home singing into the night with Johnny and Jinny arm in arm humming to the tunes, as

17

their last night together faded to memories everlasting. Solly and his wife, Beryl, walked with Taff, who was talking to his wife, Cathryn.

"It might be best if ye goes back to Wales, Cathryn."

"Why," she asked, "my friends are here?"

Beryl stopped everyone in their tracks and stamped her foot.

"What about me?" she cried. "Cathryn is my best pal. If she leaves now, I will be alone here. No, we wives must stick together and support each other. Ain't that right, Solly?"

"Thee's right, Bee, but I don't want t' interfere twixt man an' wife."

"The girls 're right, Solly," said Taff, "it was just a passing thought. I should've known better than talking wi' a belly full o' ale."

"In t' mornin' when t' men are gone," Beryl said, "we'll get Jinny to organise a tea an' cakes mornin' for t' weekend. Mebbe Sunday'll be best. Aye, what say thee, Cathryn?'

"Better 'n goin' to bloody Wales,' Cathryn replied, "an' I can show off some o' my bakin' skills."

"Good,' said Solly, "look at yonder shootin' star. Look, there's another," breaking into a chuckle. "I think that's an omen. A good one, don't ye?"

"Aye," was the chorus of three and just to reinforce the notion again, "aye."

Just then Yiggs Bliss and Billy Nolan marched past them striding out like on a Brigade of Guards route march.

"We 'aven't packed yet," Yiggs shouted. "Gonna be up all fuckin' night packin' smutter," he called back over his shoulder.

"What is smutter?" Cathryn asked.

"That's what Jews call clothing," Solly said. "Yiggs is a Jew. That's why he's still a bachelor," he added.

"Why," Beryl asked, "he's such a handsome man?"

"Cos he can't find a Jewess," said Solly.

"So what" Beryl said, "there's plenty o' lasses round here?"

"His Ma is very strict," said Solly. "She won't allow him to bring a gentile girl home."

"That's discrimination," Beryl said.

18

"No, it's not," said Solly, "it's being Jewish. Just like I won't let our daughter bring a Jew, chink, nigger or anyone I don't like the look of into our house."

"We haven't got a daughter and I'm goin' to speak to Father Kelly about your views," Beryl said.

"That'll be interesting," said Solly, "cos he taught me those views."

Further down the lane Andy and Kinney the two Scotsmen strolled along in deep thought and wondered what to say to each other as they passed a flask of whisky between them. The silence lasted quite some time until Kinney chuckled.

"Och aye, I cannae wait ta see yon feckin' Germans fly through t' feckin' sky wi' arms, legs an' heads flyin' in aw directions o'er t' feckin' battlefield."

"Aye," chuckled Andy, 'I wannae grab one o' they feckin' posh helmets as a souvenir fer Ma an' Pa. On t' feckin' mantelpiece it'll go, highly feckin' polished."

"Aye, along wi' a couple o' bayonets should look braw[4]. An' if ye gets a burglar in t' house, ye dinnae have ta go far ta feckin' see him off wi' a feckin' bayonet up his jacksie."

It was not long before the two Scots caught up with Allballs, Brummie and Tat Tudor, singing outlandish songs that should never have been heard away from the coalface. Fortunately having worked as a team in the unholy chaos of a coalmine they had bonded well over the years and knew they could depend on each other in times of great stress underground. That bond between them suddenly became tangible when the song ended and Tat proclaimed.

"As of tomorrow, our dependence on each other becomes complete. Not the usual work shift dependency down t' pit but a twenty-four hour dependency until we all come home, savvy?"

"Aye!" they all roared and strode away into the night headed for home and bed, knowing that the morrow would bring the aching loss of goodbye.

---

[4] braw - attractive

19

CHAPTER TWO

The packed train pulled into Chatham station in the late afternoon as the sun shone down on an ambulance train full of wounded soldiers going in the opposite direction. The chuffing noise of the steam trains did not prevent the sounds of the wounded emanating from the carriages.

"Christ almighty listen t' that. It sounds like they're all having their teeth pulled out. What the fuck's 'appening over there?" asked Billy.

"Red crosses on t' side means it's an ambulance train," answered Solly.

Whistles blew and lots of shouting NCOs on the station platform ordered the men out of the carriages and formed them into three ranks on the platform. The noise of shuffling boots and shouting corporals drowned the ambulance train's pitiful sounds.

"Make sure you have all of your kit. The train is leaving now!" shouted a sergeant at the head of the column. "Sling your kitbags over your right shoulder and stand to ATTEN...TION!" he roared.

The shuffling ceased momentarily as everyone stood to attention and the train let out a great belch of steam as it slowly moved and clanked out of the station, revealing the ambulance train across the tracks.

"By the front quick march!" screamed the sergeant. "Left, right, left, right!"

A lot of men had difficulty getting into step as the corporals moved along the ranks correcting them and taking their minds off the ambulance train on the platform opposite. There was much shouting.

"Eyes front! Left, right, left, right!"

The column of men marched proudly as the patriotic people of Chatham cheered them along their way to Brompton Barracks, the home of the Royal Engineers.

After just three days of crammed-in soldiering the miners were kitted out and sent off to France to begin their subterranean war against their subterranean enemy, German miners.

The troop ship rattled and banged and puked its way across the English Channel. Men lined the rails and threw up over the side. One of Sergeant Gordon's men, Taff Dupree, spewed his guts out all over a nearby officer's shiny boots. Taff could not care less. He was seasick. The officer, a captain in a cavalry regiment, flew into a rage and singled out the only NCO[5] he could see, Johnny Gordon.

"You, Sergeant! Get that man to wipe his filth off my boots. Now! Damn you."

Johnny looked at Taff, who was reaching deep into his guts and turning grey around his face. The others looked on grinning.

"Right then, Mister... erm. You need to find a tap or something with running water to wash..." Johnny said, with a remarkable effort not to grin.

"Mister! Bloody Mister. I am a captain, can't you see?" bringing his hand up to his epaulettes, pointing at the pips. "Look, you bloody fool. Three pips! You didn't even salute me. You act as though you have never seen a parade ground and you are a bloody Royal Engineers bloody Sergeant! Stand to attention when you speak to me."

"I know nowt about parade grounds and saluting and call me a fool again and thee and t' pips will be swimming. Now fuck off."

The officer's face was puce with indignation. He looked around for someone in authority. He spotted a warrant officer and immediately shouted.

"Sergeant Major Woods!"

The sergeant major responded instantly.

"Coming, sir."

The warrant officer strode across the deck and noisily slammed to attention and delivered one of those magnificent quivering

---

[5] NCO – non-commissioned officer

salutes, beloved of military martinets. Glancing past the officer at Johnny and his men his eyes admitted defeat before he could even asked the officer anything.

"This man, this sergeant, threatened to throw me over the side. Insolence and insubordination can mean a firing squad whilst on active service. Arrest him."

The nine men, including the retching Taff, quickly formed a protective circle around their sergeant, the sergeant major and the captain, all in the circle. Each of the miners had either tasted or witnessed the hard fists of their boss but this was different; pistols were about to be drawn. Solly growled menacingly. Serious injury was imminent as any consequences dissipated from the minds of the angry coal miners. The meaningful words that came from Solly's heart were like daggers to the heart of the sergeant major.

"Four days ago, we were diggin' coal down t' pit. We all volunteered to kill Germans an' if either of you two draws your fuckin' pistols I will shove it so far up thy arse you won't need to fire it to blow thy fuckin' brains out. Now just tootle off along the deck and find some fucker else to annoy."

A man of much nous and level headedness the sergeant major rounded on the captain.

"Leave this to me, sir. You go to the officers' mess; I do not want an officer present when I deal with these men."

He underlined it with another quivering salute and a stamp to attention as he turned his back on the captain and eyeballed Johnny Gordon. The captain limped away as though his foot was injured. With eyes locked onto each other the sergeant major closed the gap between them by meaningfully measuring his steps, designed to intimidate the dauntless Johnny Gordon.

"If thy face reaches my face, over t' fuckin' side tha'll go. So, stop right there."

The sergeant major stopped just an arm's length away. His gaze was resolute and his stance unyielding as he spoke succinctly in his London accent.

"A firing squad will shoot the northern shit out of you if you so much as raise your voice, let alone your arm to me or any other non-commissioned officer or commissioned officer whilst on active duty. I know your position in life and the guts it takes to perform your duties so heed what I say and die in your tunnels not in front of a firing squad and prove the northern ditty wrong."

"Which northern ditty might that be?" asked Johnny.

"Northern born, northern bred. Thick in t' arm and thick in t' fuckin' head," replied the sergeant major, mimicking a north country accent.

"If we are digging tunnels for the like of thee, the firing squad might be the lesser of the two evils," said Sergeant Johnny Gordon.

Thus began the Great War for the men from the hills and dales of Great Britain; or more correct to say, from beneath the hills and dales of Great Britain.

CHAPTER THREE

On arrival at Le Havre the troopship spewed its cargo onto the dock where organised chaos was taking place with soldiers running to and fro and groups of men being shouted at and herded hither and thither to form up before boarding a train. Not any old train. No this train was a long line of cattle trucks where wild-eyed horses were dragged up ramps into the wagons.

The Royal Engineers contingent drifted out of harm's way and gathered in the shade of a long shed where they split into their small groups and immediately lit up ciggies, unsure of what would happen next. Johnny kept his men close as they enjoyed their cigarettes. Marching toward them a captain and sergeant major soon made their presence felt as the latter shouted.

"Get those fags out and fall in! Three ranks. Quickly! Fucking move!"

With a certain amount of bewilderment the men quickly formed into three ranks facing the newcomers.

"Get those rifles into the shoulder and pick up your kitbags," shouted the sergeant major. "You are now on active service so listen carefully to your commanding officer, Captain Tweedy."

Captain Tweedy checked his watch and pointed to the cattle trucks just across the dock.

"Sorry about the transport, but it's that or marching and I am not marching anywhere." Looking at the troopship he said, "I hear some of you had a problem with a cavalry officer on board the *Queen Alexandra*. Something about being seasick all over his boots?" He gazed along the three ranks of forty men, "I must inform you now, should any such nonsense occur from this moment on, I will shoot you on the spot. Now form into your sections for the roll call."

The men shuffled to separate into their sections of ten men with their NCOs in the front rank. The sergeant major called out names from his sheet of paper.

"Stand to attention and call out yes sir when you hear your name."

The stamping of boots and yes sir was heard forty times, followed by a silence disturbed only by the scavenging seagulls and moans of newly arrived wounded being carried onto the *Queen Alexandra* for the journey home to England.

"All present and correct, sir."

"Very good, Sergeant Major Scragg. Please get them aboard the train while I find the quartermaster," he then pointed at Johnny. "You, Sergeant, come with me. Leave your kit with your men."

Johnny dropped his kit and slung his rifle over his shoulder and followed Captain Tweedy across the dock to where gangs of Chinese coolies[6] worked with all kinds of military hardware, seemingly knowing what went in whatever designated pile. The men in uniform were all senior NCOs and each was shouting at various Chinese gang bosses who in turn shouted at their men to pick whatever up and load it onto the cattle trucks.

"Q!" shouted Captain Tweedy.

A tall thin man, a WO2[7], saluted and marched across to meet them.

"Hello, sir, we've about got everything we ordered and we're just finishing loading it on the train," said SQMS[8] Cuthbert Williams, a Welshman aged about forty years.

"Jolly good, Q, and I've got forty new tunnellers to use it. Do you need help here before I put them on the train?"

"No, sir, my Chinks like to think it's their job to handle stores and those boys will need a rest after being on that tub for the last eight hours," he said looking at Johnny. "Who're you, Sergeant?"

"Johnny Gordon."

"All right Sergeant Gordon, when you speak to me you call me Q, savvy?"

---

[6] Chinese coolies – indentured labourers

[7] WO2 – warrant officer second class

[8] SQMS - Squadron Quartermaster Sergeant, a staff sergeant appointment in traditionally mounted regiments and corps of the British Army

"Savvy, Q," replied Johnny.

"I like a man of few words. We'll get on well when you know the ropes. Where're you from?"

"Bold Heath, Q."

"Bold fucking Heath! Where the fuck's that?"

"Twixt St Helens and Widnes, Q, Lancashire," replied Johnny.

"A Lancashire lad, eh. Tha'll be reet cosy under t' French clay, lad," said Cuthbert Williams in a mocking Lancashire accent.

"Aye, Q, I can't wait to get down t' hole and blow fucking Germans t' sky."

"Thee 'n me'll get on champion, lad but we don't call them Germans. They're Jerry, Bosch, Fritz or Huns and forget Christmas footballs between the trenches and carol singing to each other, that's horseshit. Kill the bastards, that's why we're here."

Captain Tweedy intervened.

"Get back to your men Sergeant Gordon, and try to rest. I will join you presently. Tell your men to rest and sleep if possible, there will be no sleeping tonight, you'll be digging."

"We'll be needin' good grub, Captain Tweedy, an' plenty of ..."

"Address me as sir, Sergeant Gordon, and your needs are already taken care of. Please expedite my orders so I don't feel the need to repeat myself, and salute as you do so."

Humiliation is a feeling Johnny rarely experienced and Captain Tweedy did not miss the flash of anger in Johnny's eyes as he performed the sloppiest of salutes and stalked off without another word. Johnny made his way along the train to where his men beckoned him from a cattle wagon and he climbed aboard to join them.

"Right, lads, listen up! We're goin' straight down t' 'ole from this train, so make yourselves comfy an' get some kip. The food..."

"How the fuck can we kip wi' all this horseshit on t' floor?" interjected Billy Nolan. "It's fuckin' drenched wi' piss as well," he whined.

"C'mon, we'll find a clean wagon," ordered Johnny.

26

They all climbed out of the cattle truck in search of another when Sgt Major Scragg roared.

"Where the fuck is you lot going? Get back in that fucking wagon right now. Fucking deserting before you've even fired a fucking shot will get you all a fucking firing squad. Get back in there!"

"You fuckin' get in there an' lie in horseshit an' piss if you like. I fuckin' don't," shouted Billy Nolan.

"Be quiet, Billy," said Johnny as the others started to mouth off.

"There is men in trenches 'd give their right arm to be lying in horseshit right now. They're lying in blood and shit and praying for their lives and guess what? They're waiting for you to relieve them, so move your fucking arses and get back in there now!"

"This next one is cleaner," shouted Solly

"That wagon and all the ones behind it are going to a different battlefield. How many times must I waste my fucking breath? Get on the fucking train!"

Johnny took over.

"Climb aboard lads. Chuck your kit on t' floor an' kip on it."

The men climbed back into the wagon as Sgt Major Scragg beckoned Johnny to join him. The two men looked into each other's eyes, neither of them intimidated by the other as they met alongside the train.

"You are a sergeant in the Royal Engineers and you are going into battle with other Royal Engineers who have earned their stripes through due diligence and years of service. You and your men will get the shock of your lives when you leave this train and I expect you to control them and get them digging out of sight of every fucking officer on the front line. Discipline means everything to the officer class and men get shot for insubordination on the front line, savvy?"

"Savvy, Sgt Major Scragg. But I'm not their fucking keeper, am I?"

"Oh, yes you fucking are. And call me, sir when you address me. You are their fucking God from now on and you'll need to be tougher here than at the coalface."

"No disrespect, sir, but what does thee know about down t' pit?"

Scragg looked into Johnny's eyes but saw neither smugness nor malice, just an honest sky blue-eyed question.

"Not as much as thee, Sergeant, but in the pits you're about to go down I know much more than thee so get back to your men and get some sleep. Hot grub and a tot o' rum are at the end of this line, then down t' pit you go."

The noise of the horses and the clanking train seemed to lull the men to sleep rather than prevent it. Some of them lay awake as wagons noisily uncoupled in the waning light of the late summer evening then fell asleep again as the train moved off. Yiggs Bliss looked up at the stars and elbowed Tat Tudor.

"I've never seen so many shooting stars in one night, Tat, have you?"

Tat grunted and rolled onto his back to look skywards.

"Not sure if them's fuckin' stars mate. They ain't far enough away for my liking. But I wish they was."

The penny dropped for Yiggs.

"Fuckin' 'ell! Them's fuckin' artillery shells; how the fuck far are they goin'? Must be a dozen miles or more. Jeez, what the fuck 'ave we volunteered for?"

The innocent looking streaks of light in the sky shocked Yiggs and his talk incited the others to question their being there. Billy sat up and studied the night sky.

"If that is what I think it is, it's fuckin' rainin' artillery shells o'er there an' o'er 'ere, which fuckin' battlefield are we goin' to, that one or that fucker o'er there?'

Concerned for the morale of his men Johnny shouted at Billy.

"What have I told thee about t' cakehole? Shut it an' keep it shut an' get t' head back down in t' horseshit."

The men looked at each other, searching for that inkling of fear they all felt, while hoping they had suppressed their own trepidation enough to be hidden from their comrades. With these men testosterone needed to be stronger than adrenaline because this was the world of the warrior, whether they fought Germans or the coalface they must win. Unlike the Spanish bullfighter haughtily strutting around a dead bull celebrating a victory, these men shunned such theatrical antics and deemed it unworthy, unless on the football field.

Eventually the train stopped and they all began to stir and sit up. Realising that this was the end of the line, Johnny gave his first orders to his men. The darkness seemed to enhance the authority behind the voice, as in the distance exploding artillery shells lit up the night sky.

"Make sure you have all your kit and stay by me. No yapping or smoking 'til I say so."

The noise of scraping metal was heard as the side opening of the wagon dropped open and Sgt Major Scragg beckoned them out onto a railway sidings platform.

"Be careful of the wounded on your way to that lorry over there," he stage-whispered.

The wounded men lying on stretchers covered practically every inch of the sprawling platform, hundreds of them, some silent, some moaning in pain. Leading his men Johnny deftly crept through the lines of stretchers. His men close on his heels headed for the lorry where a sergeant beckoned then greeted them.

"Good to see new blood, lads. Straight in t' lorry and mind you don't do t' splits on t' old blood on t' floor," he said, grinning broadly, "and I be Sergeant Bennett, your section commander."

"That's my job," said Johnny, "these are my men."

Sgt Bennett noticed Johnny's three chevrons and followed the line of his arm up into the steel cut face where the blue eyes shone under the peak of his forage cap.

"My mistake matey," holding his hand out for a shake, "Joe Bennett, all t' way from Widnes in Lancashire."

Johnny shook his hand.

"Johnny Gordon. We're all from around Widnes, Bold Heath and Sutton Manor. We were all down t' pit four days ago. How long's thee been here?"

29

"Since start last year. I'm a regular, done ten years, an' here's thee with three stripes in four days. Fuckin' hell, is thee related t' King?"

"Aye, old King Coal, the merry old soul. One day matey, not four. I got fuckin' stripes on t' first day. Stripes was on t' uniform waitin' for me. Hellfire Jack ordered..."

"Hellfire fuckin' Jack? The brass is shitting sandbags cos he's comin' here tomorrow."

"Brass, what's that?" asked Johnny.

"Fuckin' officers. You got some learnin' to do matey. Come 'n see me if you're in a pickle, we're in t' same company."

"Which is?" asked Johnny.

"174th Tunnelling Company, Royal Engineers, an' we're headin' for Albert, not far from here. Scraggy'll be in t' cab wi' me, y' see, I'm t' driver so try to get comfy. You've got hot grub and a tot o' rum waitin' for ye."

Sgt Major Scragg arrived and secured the tailboard with Joe Bennett's help. No words were exchanged and the two men went to the front of the lorry and climbed into the cab. A low crunching of gears and a jerky start and off they went to rear echelon[9] HQ in the French town of Albert. In the back of the lorry the men sat on wooden benches and smoked cigarettes as they groused about feeling every bump in the road - military vehicles have solid rubber tyres, hence the nickname boneshakers.

"Sithee, our Johnny," said Billy Nolan, "we're supposed to be restin', not shakin' an' bouncin' around afore we goes down t' pit."

"Two things to remember, all of you," said Johnny, "I'm not our Johnny or any other fuckin' Johnny and from now on ye call me Sarge, especially when t' officers are in earshot, savvy?"

"Aye, Johnny, we savvy," the chorus echoed in the darkness of the lorry and they chuckled amongst themselves.

The lorry entered the town of Albert and jarred the bones of the men in the rear as it rolled over the cobblestone streets. It stopped

---

[9] rear echelon - the section of an army concerned with administrative and supply duties

and the engine cut to silence. Moments later the tailboard was quietly lowered by Sgt Joe Bennett.

"Be as quiet as ye can," he stage-whispered, "miners are sleeping nearby."

The men silently passed their kit down to each other then climbed down from the lorry.

"Follow me," said Joe Bennett, "hot grub an' a tot o' rum is waitin' for ye in t' billet o'er yonder. Sithee, in t' corner t' courtyard."

They followed him through a heavy curtain and along a candlelit passageway into a large room where there was a long table laden with dixies[10] full of steaming meat stew and a tea urn behind which stood a burly corporal holding a heavy metal ladle. Rows of metal cups were on a nearby table next to a pile of long loaves of bread, cut into large chunks.

"One piece of bread and two cups, one for t' stew an' t' other for t' tea an' rum," said the corporal, "look after t' cups, they're yours, so keep 'em clean an' don't lose 'em. Now line up in front of me for t' stew an' tea. Rum is your pudding after t' tea."

The men sat on wooden benches to eat off large tables. The warm French bread and the hot meat stew altered the mood of the men as they enjoyed their first meal on the Western Front. The men finished eating and they all looked at the corporal.

"You don't think I'm putting on a pinny an' fuckin' servin' ye, do ye?" said the corporal, "Fuckin" get up here an' finish the horse stew afore I dish out the rum."

A moment of silence then they chorused.

"Fucking horse!"

"Aye, fuckin' 'orse," said the corporal, "what the fuck do you expect, prime fuckin' beef? It be fresh meat from yonder battlefield. Hundreds of 'em get killed every day so we eat 'em. Ye didnae think we fuckin' bury 'em did ye?"

"First time I've ate horse," said Solly, "it wuz better 'n some butchers' meat I've tasted."

---

[10] dixie - a large metal pot for cooking, brewing tea

"That don't surprise me," said Yiggs Bliss. "Liverpool butchers chop up dogs 'n fuckin' cats 'n fuck knows what else."

"How the fuck does thee know owt about Liverpool," said Solly, "you've never been there you fuckin' woolyback?"

"No, but I've met enough fuckin' scousers to know. Yers are like a fuckin' rash, yers get everywhere," said Yiggs.

Just then an officer entered the room.

"Feedin' t' men afore they go down t' 'ole, sir," said the corporal, "ten minutes an' they're ready, sir."

"Very good, Corporal," said the officer as he faced the men.

"My name is Captain Richardson. I am your commanding officer and I am here to greet you and tell you about your task."

Looking around the murky room he saw the stripes on Johnny's arm.

"Ah, there you are, Sgt Gordon. Please stand when I address you."

Johnny got to his feet.

"Thank you," said the captain.

"I know all of you have not had the military training required of the British army, but I still require the basics of military behaviour." He looked Johnny in the eye and said, "It takes many years of hard work and discipline to become a Royal Engineers sergeant, Sgt Gordon, and here you are just four days into your service wearing the chevrons of a senior non-commissioned officer. A sergeant, no less."

"Not of my choosing," said Johnny. "Hellfire Jack ordered this, not me. I don't need stripes to get the best out of my men, so maybe I should remove 'em. I hear he's coming here in t' mornin' so I'll give 'em back in t' mornin' unless you want 'em now?"

"That will not be necessary, Sgt Gordon," said the captain, "I trust my real soldiers will correct you as time goes by. We'll soon see what you're made of."

"You said something about our task," said Johnny.

"Ah yes, you are about to relieve a section of sappers working on Lochnagar Street. The entrance has been dug to a new tunnel and the shaft is ninety feet deep. The main gallery is under construction now, which is going to be three hundred yards long and lined with timber as you go. Sergeant Bennett will be here shortly to take you to work. He will be with you to familiarise you with the task, so do exactly as he tells you and remember, complete silence. The Hun must never discover our position."

The captain about turned and walked out.

"Come an' get your rum," growled the corporal as he lifted a large stone jar into view, "only sappers get this so don't mention it to t' Chinks an' infantry down t' 'ole."

Joe Bennett entered the room.

"Ah, just in time for t' rum. Five minutes lads a' we're goin' down t' 'ole. T' other shift are just comin' out."

"Where're they goin' Joe?" asked Johnny.

"Back to t' billet in t' village, Johnny. They're over t' moon cos you lot are here. Back to t' eight hour shifts now instead of twelve. Fuckin' hard work is twelve hours down t' 'ole."

"So, we're doin' t' night shift. For how long?" asked Johnny.

"Can't say, mate. But the longer the better cos you get best grub 'n rum an' you see daylight. T' others are down t' 'ole all day an' come out in t' night, they don't see t' sun at all, but now you're here the six 'til two shift an' the two 'til ten shifts'll get an hour or two of sun. You lads'll be on ten 'til six shift so even if you're on trench repair gang you'll get plenty of sun."

"Trench repair gang," said Johnny, "what's that?"

"War, Johnny. It's fuckin' war. Shells smash us to bits every day an' some fucker 'as to fix the smashed trenches so we can shoot back at Jerry. Don't worry, t' infantry does the shootin' while we does the diggin' so c'mon, sup up, time to go."

The men grabbed their kitbags but Joe Bennett snapped.

"Leave all that here, bring only your cups an' rifles. Don't worry no bugger'll touch it. Yers can pick it up at t' end o' t' shift. Oh, and it be tin hats from now so put 'em on."

The night sky lit up with flashes and bangs as artillery shells passed each other on their way to their various German and British targets. Joe Bennett led the men along a path, which soon turned into a slushy slope and then became duck-boarded trenches zigzagging through the French countryside toward the front line. The going was slow and precarious as the sappers squeezed past infantrymen manning the trenches. They arrived at a place where the trench ran deeper and formed a junction with another trench that ran underground.

"This is a Russian sap," said Joe Bennett. "It's a concealed communication trench for the movement of men and equipment that Jerry can't see, so no bugger gets killed in here, unless a shell hits it."

"Where's it going?" asked Johnny.

"T' front line and t' other tunnels," replied Joe.

"This is Lochnagar Street where we have several tunnels on the go. We've been diggin' 'ere for months now and so has Jerry, but he doesn't know about our tunnels. Y' see, we work silently on t' cross."

"On t' fuckin' cross, what the fuck's that?" asked Johnny as the others gathered round.

"Yers'll see in a minute when we gets t' face, an' remember, no fuckin' talkin' an' no fuckin' noise. Jerry don't know we're 'ere an' its gotta stay that way, savvy?"

They all nodded in enthusiastic agreement and moved on until they reached another timber clad entrance with a miniature railway line running out of it and along Lochnagar Street into the murky darkness ahead. Joe halted the sappers as a rubble-laden trolley pushed by a Chinese labourer emerged from the tunnel and quietly trundled away out of sight along Lochnagar Street.

"Chinks get rid t' spoil so don't get in t' way an' never speak to 'em," Joe whispered.

Following the railway lines down a gentle slope they arrived at the shaft-head chamber and saw that they needed to climb down a ladder trussed to the top rim of tubbing - this was a circular section of steel cladding going vertically down into the earth, each section bolted to each other descending to ninety feet. Above them was a

34

robust rig of lifting gear to haul up the trolleys of spoil; it sat motionless during shift changes. At any other time it would have been a hive of silent activity lowering empty trolleys and lifting full ones out of the tunnel. Chinese coolies not soldiers did this arduous work.

Johnny went first and mounted the rim by grabbing the ladder and stepping on the box step and pulled himself up to stand on the rim. Before descending he looked at his men, pursed his lips and touched them with his forefinger.

"Shhh," he said, as he disappeared down the shaft.

With his head bowed looking down between his feet he saw the bottom of the ladder slightly offset from the next ladder, which was firmly trussed to the legs and bottom rung of the one he was on. Adjusting his gait with a slight lean to his right he was on the next ladder and descending fast to the next ladder and so on to the bottom of the shaft, from where he looked up to see his men silently climbing down toward him. Climbing down this dark hole would be challenging for most men but for miners this was just another route to get to work.

At the bottom of the shaft they arrived at a large area cut out of the clay where stacks of timber and railway lines were stored along with the paraphernalia of mining. Johnny gathered his men and waited for the last man down, Joe Bennett. The air down there was quite different from up top. It felt cool and clammy with a slight metallic taste. Joe Bennett did not miss the distasteful looks and stage-whispered.

"New blowers will be installed this week. They came with you lot, on t' same ship."

"Thank fuck for that," whispered Solly. "When thee goes back up, Sarge, check t' exhaust is well away from t' intake."

"Right-o," whispered Joe Bennett. "When thee gets three stripes like me 'n Johnny, I might heed what ye says, 'til then, fuckin' shut up. Now follow me."

There was a wooden hut with a light shining out of its door where the silhouette of a large man could be seen moving about inside. Joe Bennett halted the men and whispered in the doorway. The man inside, a warrant officer, stepped out and introduced himself by whispering.

"I am WO2 Connor and if I tell you to do something you do it instantly. Who's in charge?"

"Me," whispered Johnny, "Johnny Gordon, from Bold Heath near Widnes."

"Which pub do you use, the Ring O Bells or the Griffin?" asked WO2 Connor.

"The Griffin, but how the fuck does thee know t' Griffin an t' Ring O Bells?"

WO2 Connor grinned and whispered.

"You probably know my twin brother, Arthur Connor. He stayed home and lives in Pit Lane but I joined t' army years ago. D' you knows him? I'm his brother, Jimmy Connor," they all nodded and grinned that they knew him. "Good, now off to work with you, and you, Johnny, come back here to my office when you're ready, I'll make a brew."

Quietly the sappers shuffled off down the tunnel, pressing themselves against the timber walls when Chinese coolies approached pushing their trolleys. Further on down the gradient the trolley lines ended where the spoil was piled ready for shovelling into the sandbags then loaded onto the trolleys.

Joe Bennett beckoned the men forward to where the tools lay on the clay floor in front of the face to be dug. Grabbing a cross-shaped piece of timber, he placed it so it connected at the roof with the roof timbers. He then grabbed a spade and with his back on the cross, demonstrated silent digging by shoving the spade with his feet using the cross-shaped timber as the backrest.

The blade of the spade was sharp and designed to cut through the clay enabling the digger to extract clods of earth. The digger's feet did all the work silently pushing the spade into the clay face, while his mate grabbed the clod and passed it back to the next man who put it on the pile ready for bagging and loading onto the trolley.

As the face was dug, the setts[11] were installed every nine inches of cut out face, making the roof and sides safe from collapse. A sett consisted of four pieces of wood: a sole for the floor, two legs for each side, and a cap for the roof - because of the need for silent working no nails or screws were used. The sole and cap planks were cut with small rebated steps which located the legs to the cap and sole so that the pressure of the clay was all that was required to hold the sett firmly in place. The men handled the timbers to satisfy their curiosity as Joe continued digging.

Demonstration over, Joe got off the cross and passed the spade to Solly who deftly mounted the cross and started his first cut into French soil. Kinney grabbed the clod of clay and passed it back to Yiggs who handed it to Andy to place on the pile ready for bagging. On the other side of the pile, Billy Nolan, Brummie and Tat Tudor arranged the timber setts ready to install as Taff and Allballs examined the trolley rails. Johnny looked on taking it all in. Satisfied, he whispered to Taff.

"Rotate every twenty minutes and fit the sett every nine inches and don't overfill the trolleys. I'll be back soon."

He beckoned Joe Bennett and headed for Jimmy Connor's shack, Joe close on his heels as they crouched low and silently scurried along the tunnel. Warrant Officer Connor beckoned the two sergeants into his underground shed in the cavernous stores area.

"C'mon, brew'll be cold in a minute and there's a lot of tidyin' up afore Hellfire Jack comes in t' morning."

"When's he coming?" Johnny asked.

"Fuck knows, but we've got to be on t' ball. He's no fuckin' pushover and we need to know afore he gets here how much railway line have we got and sandbags an' fuckin' setts. He don't tolerate fuck ups, especially if it's about lack of equipment. So, we'll check everything after t' brew."

Ten minutes later, Johnny and Joe were stacking the miniature railway lines neatly in stacks of ten.

---

[11] setts - timber planks ready cut to size; pit props

37

"Fuckin' hell, there's nearly a fuckin' mile of track here," said Joe.

"Aye, and we're nowhere near done yet. Hellfire Jack plans to link up wi' t' Paris fuckin' Metro," laughed Johnny.

"Ye didn't let on ye'd been to Paris."

"I 'aven't, but I read the newspapers, an' I intend goin' there, Joe."

"Praps I'll come wi' ye."

"Yeah, we'll see t' Eiffel Tower an' t' Folies Bergére."

"Fuckin' hell,' said Joe, "we'll 'ave a right rip-a-knicker night."

They smothered their giggles as Jimmy Connor appeared.

"What's so fuckin' funny?" he asked. "Here we are in Satan's arsehole an' you two are fuckin' laughing."

"Me 'n Johnny's goin' t' Paris, Q," said Joe.

"Oh, I'll order bigger fuckin' shovels then, should I?" said Jimmy Connor, with a wry smile on his face.

The men stifled their laughter.

"There's a brew on for t' lads so send them back four at a time. We can't stop diggin' at t' face. Go get 'em Johnny."

Johnny scampered away to get half of his men, leaving Joe and Jimmy Connor stacking railway lines.

Throughout the night the men worked hard like miners do and there was no thanks for their effort apart from the brews and hot soup provided by WO2 Connor, the quartermaster of the Tunnelling Company.

The men cleared the debris and made ready for the incoming shift just as Hellfire Jack arrived. The bedraggled men tried in vain to pick off lumps of clay stuck to their tunics and their faces. Johnny saluted Hellfire Jack who returned the salute.

"How far have you dug, Sgt Gordon?' he asked.

Johnny wiped his brow.

"I'm not sure, sir, but we placed eight setts."

"Bloody good show, especially on your first shift underground." Turning to face Joe Bennett he said, "Get those men ready to go back and wait for me at the shaft." Turning back to Johnny, he said, "Show me your setts. Let's see how good you are."

Crouching low they moved along the tunnel. Tiny alcoves cut into the sides of the tunnel held oil lamps and candles to provide the poor light along their way. In just a few minutes they arrived at the clay face where Hellfire Jack saw the new section of railway line laid and secured with no debris at all – a welcome sight for the incoming shift, not that there is anything welcoming about this terrible place.

"Jolly good show, Sgt Gordon. You've certainly earned your stripes where it matters most. Now let's get back to the quartermaster's shed."

Jimmy Connor was alone in his shed when Hellfire Jack and Johnny arrived.

"Have you told the men about getting back to their billet, Q?"

"No, sir, I expect Sgt Bennett will tell them before they leave the shaft."

"Right, listen, Sgt Gordon. When you leave the shaft you will see terrible things on your journey through what I can only describe as a bloody battlefield. Going back to your billet you will see many wounded and dead soldiers. You will also be a target for Jerry snipers, so keep your heads down and never try to see what is going on outside any of the trenches you are about to go through. Also, do not get into conversation with infantrymen. Sometimes they get captured and will tell all when tortured."

Having witnessed broken bodies and severed limbs in the coalmine Johnny seemed quite unperturbed. However, in just a little while his outlook on life was to change dramatically. Joining his men at the shaft he imparted Hellfire Jack's message and tapped his helmet.

"Tin hats stay on heads 'til I says otherwise and stick close to each other and no fuckin' talking. C'mon, lets get out of here."

On the way out they met the relief shift coming in - lots of grins and nods of unsure recognition, but total silence. A sentry stepped aside to allow them into Lochnagar Street, the shallow tunnel leading to the trenches and battlefields of France.

Trudging through Lochnagar Street the sounds of exploding shells seemed far away, but then, as they approached the open trenches the chatter of machine gun fire got louder and louder and the whizz-bang noise of overhead shelling created the sensation of a banging tambourine inside their heads.

Lochnagar Street ended at right angles to the trench and in the mouth of the tunnel several bodies lay with just enough room to walk into daylight between them. Some were headless while others were mangled flesh and tunic, totally unrecognisable. Johnny stepped into the river of blood on the tunnel floor before stepping out into daylight. The men followed him, everyone stunned into silence by the sight and sounds of trench warfare. Joe Bennett scrambled past the men to get to Johnny.

"I'll lead the way, mate. Make sure ye sees where we're going cos I'm not with you tonight," he shouted.

"Fuckin' hell, Joe. Where are ye going?" asked Johnny.

"I'm bringing a fresh shift on at two o'clock. Thee relieves me at ten o'clock tonight so bed your men down after breakfast. Yers'll need a good kip. Ain't life a bucket of shit."

Johnny looked back at his men who were all crouched in the trench.

"Stay close," he shouted, "and don't fuckin' stop for ought, even if you're fuckin' shot, keep moving."

Joe scampered ahead with Johnny close on his heels but glanced back every couple of seconds. He saw the fear in his men's eyes and hoped they could not see his. The trenches were built in a zigzag formation so every few seconds there was a change in direction; a turn to the right or the left and Johnny momentarily lost sight of his men as he rounded each corner traversing the battlefield. He tended to raise himself up to see his men but that soon stopped when a fragment of shrapnel ricocheted off his tin hat.

The going was really rough as they scrambled over collapsed trench walls where the rubble lay on the wooden duckboards. The protruding limbs of dead soldiers stuck out grotesquely and bloody dead faces gazed up as they strode over them. Joe halted at a

40

junction where a wooden sign read Manchester pointing one way and Liverpool pointing the other.

"Remember that," said Joe, emphatically.

Joe strode over a corpse and led them away from the maelstrom of exploding artillery shells and machine gun fire, but the threat still lay in the air as shells whined overhead on their dreadful way to destroy whatever was in their path.

After nearly an hour of ducking and diving among the trenches, and avoiding the never ending flow of stretcher bearers carrying their unfortunate cargoes to what is known as the Casualty Clearing Area in the rear, eventually Johnny and his men arrived at their billet on the outskirts of a village, which had suffered much shelling but was still usable for billeting soldiers. The men dragged their feet across the courtyard and into the canteen - their kit remained perched on the wooden benches where they had left them the night before.

"Line up for t' breakfast," shouted the burly corporal as he stirred a steaming dixie."

"I 'ears you lot earned your breakfast last night," he added.

"News travels fast round 'ere, mate," said Johnny.

"Aye, but can yers keep it up? That's what matters round 'ere?" said the corporal.

"How long have ye been cooking?" asked Johnny.

"Half an hour, why?"

"So that's last night's grub warmed up, yeah?"

"You might say that; we keeps adding to it every day an' chuck it out when it gets a bit whiffy. Why?"

Johnny pointed at the open door where fresh rations were kept in what must be the larder.

"You've got eggs out there, I can see 'em," he said.

"Them's for t' staff," snapped the corporal.

"What staff?"

"The HQ staff in the offices. The Chief Clerk and his staff and the officers…"

"And you," interrupted Johnny.

"Well, you don't think I'm gonna leave myself out, do you?"

Johnny nodded at Taff.

"Get two eggs each from that basket in there an' put a pan of water on t' boil."

The burly corporal stood to his full height and waved the ladle at Johnny.

"Hiding behind your stripes, are you? Why not get the eggs yourself?"

In a flash, Johnny leaped over the makeshift counter and ducked as the ladle swiped by his head. The burly corporal moved fast for a big man and managed to parry some of Johnny's punches but he was no match for Johnny's fast, hard fists. He was unconscious before he hit the floor when Johnny connected with a left and right to the jaw.

Joe Bennett walked in and remonstrated with Johnny.

"What the fuck happened 'ere you fuckin' idiot?"

"Call me an idiot again, Joe, and thee'll join him," rasped Johnny.

"You could be shot for doing this mate. C'mon, wake him up afore t' brass comes in."

Solly and Yiggs grabbed the corporal's shoulders and sat him upright.

"Get some water," shouted Yiggs, as he glared at the others, "fuckin' hurry up."

Allballs and Andy dashed to the sink and filled their mugs with cold water and threw it at the corporal, splashing onto Yiggs. The following silence broke as the others laughed at the dripping Yiggs. The laughter ceased abruptly as an officer marched in and Joe Bennett shouted.

"Shun!"

The officer took everything in but did not break his stride as he marched straight into the larder and returned with a couple of apples. He spoke without stopping.

"Laughter is good for the soul, haven't heard it for months. I see the corporal's been at the rum again. Sort him out Sgt Bennett, before anyone else sees him, there's a good chap."

They all looked at each other in amazement.

"Who the fuck was that?" asked Johnny.

"Freddie Spence, Mister Spence to you mate. He's our Troop Commander. He'll be a captain soon, an' a bloody good 'un."

"What's a Troop Commander?" asked Johnny.

"He is boss of a troop. A troop is four sections of men, you an' your lads are a section. A sergeant; a corporal an' eight men, one of 'em might be a lance corporal, so you need to select two of your lads to be a corporal and a lance corporal soon."

"I thought you said there's three shifts, which means three sections are working the shifts. Where does the fourth section work?" asked Johnny.

"There are three field sections, which is what we are, and an HQ section, which does all kinds of work around our positions," pointing at the burly corporal he said, "like him. He's in HQ section and the others have various jobs around here. Don't think they get it easy. They don't and we rely on them for all kinds of things, even though we call them handbags."

The corporal started to come around and was quickly awake and getting to his feet.

"What we gonna do about him?" asked Johnny.

"I'll give him a bollocking now for striking a senior NCO," said Joe. "He'll shit his self if 'e thinks I'll report him." Joe slapped a friendly hand on Johnny's shoulder, "C'mon, get this meat down yer guts, yer gonna need it."

"I prefer the eggs," snapped Johnny.

"Believe me, Johnny, eggs is good but doesn't beat good English horsemeat. I'll get you eggs but yer blokes'll suffer down t' 'ole."

"Okay, Joe, we'll go with the meat, but thee make sure yon' fat twat don't spit in our grub."

Joe chuckled as the incident came to its meaty end with a sulking corporal morosely stirring the horsemeat stew. The men were in better spirits when fresh warm bread arrived carried in by one of the handbags.

The men were billeted in a nearby house, which had been hit by artillery shells but the cellar was intact and spacious. Part of the cellar was used as a store with stacks of stretchers, some of which were used as beds propped up on bricks to keep them off the floor. Johnny and his men slept fitfully because of artillery shells exploding in the distance. This noisy situation soon became part of life on the Western Front for all soldiers who lived long enough to get used to it. Hundreds of thousands of troops did not. They died in droves in an area called no man's land as this terrible war rolled on and Johnny and his men tried to sleep.

Allballs and Brummie lay head to head whispering to each other.

"Is thee frit yet?" whispered Allballs.

"Frit! I'm frightened shitless since we left Lochnagar Street,' replied Brummie.

"All those dead faces lookin' at me as I stepped o'er them," said Allballs, "right put willies up me. I cannae get 'em outta my mind, fuckin' dreadful."

"Aye, and this is only our first fuckin' day," said Brummie, "and this mornin' was t' first time Jesus Christ entered my head since I was a kid."

The clammy atmosphere in the cellar seemed to carry the whispers to every corner and the others held their breath to listen. Johnny's voice broke the atmosphere.

"Was Jesus carrying a pick?"

"Why?" replied Brummie.

"Cos he'd need one to get inside thy fuckin' head."

Guffaws of laughter erupted in the cellar dissipating the nervousness in a jiffy. Billy sat upright on his camp bed and chuckled.

"Jesus'd need dynamite for Brummie's head."

"Shut up, Billy," said Johnny, "thee farted all t' way through t' trenches so be quiet."

More laughter.

The terrible days and nights passed quickly in a daze of explosions during daylight hours and subterranean digging at night. During their shifts underground the men had to take turns at listening posts dug into the sides of tunnels to enable them to hear enemy miners digging in their area.

The listening sentry would crouch in the hole in numbing silence, trying to detect sounds and wondering whether or not he was hearing things in his vivid imagination. That hole could very quickly become his grave if Jerry blew a nearby mine, caving in any tunnels in the vicinity, which often happened. If the listening sentry thought he could hear something one of his tools was a sharpened stake that he would insert into the clay and clamp his teeth onto it. Any vibrations of earthworks would be felt through his teeth. Many dark lonely hours were spent relying on teeth to detect the enemy. Hours of breathing foul air and damp, if not wet, conditions broke down the health of many miners.

Solly eased his legs out in front of him to get more comfortable, which was difficult even for small men and Solly was the biggest man in the section. Like most miners Solly was a strong, hard man and rarely did he show any emotion. He hid his feelings behind grim silence or noisy laughter; but here, alone under no man's land in a narrow claustrophobic tunnel his mind played awful tricks on him because he was only human after all. After thirty minutes of stunning silence and racing adrenaline, combined with a vivid imagination, Solly was streaming with sweat in this cold, damp grave, which his mind kept telling him was where he was.

"Oh, dear Lord of the universe, I beseech thee to save my soul from this evil Hell in which I now lie. Glory be to you great Lord."

He held his breath for a moment - listening, listening.

"What the fuck's that?" he thought, as he heard something moving coming towards him.

His heartbeat was like a drum in his skull as he raised the Webley pistol and pointed it between his feet along the narrow tunnel. He did not realise he was holding his breath until he let it go when he saw that it was Kinney approaching to relieve him in the darkness.

"Thank you, Father. You heard my prayer."

Kinney, being a small man, approached on his hands and knees, which was difficult whilst holding a tiny cage with a canary in it. His body in the narrow passage blocked out the poor light from a nearby candle. Solly realised he was being relieved so he squeezed further back into the enlarged cavity designed for shift changes where men can pass each other in the confined space of this horrible death trap. In the darkness Solly took the birdcage and carefully placed it in a tiny cut out ledge in the wall of the tunnel. He saw the fear in Kinney's eyes as they met and wondered what Kinney could see in his eyes. It mattered not because both men knew. Without doubt they were filled with abject terror each and every time they entered the listening post tunnels to lie in wait for the unsuspecting enemy who, not surprisingly, came along only too often. When this happened the bile boiled in the guts of these utterly courageous soldiers. Talking was forbidden in these lonely outposts but Kinney ignored the rules and whispered.

"I've brought a wee friend wi' me cos gas has leaked into yon big gallery next door an' it's nay far from here."

With their faces practically touching as they squeezed past each other Solly whispered.

"All's quiet here so mind ye don't fall asleep. Yon canary'll not wake thee up if gas comes along here, it'll just drop dead."

"Aye, but I just listen to the silence, it's music to me," said Kinney.

"If ye hears Chopin's *Sonata No. 2 in B-Flat Minor* check the fuckin' canary an' start fuckin' crawlin' outta here. 'Ere, take the pistol, I need some fresh air."

Kinney grabbed the pistol and asked.

"I did nae' ken ye was a music buff, Solly."

"I ain't, but I knows the fuckin' *Funeral March* when I 'ears it."

Solly blocked out all the light as he disappeared along the listening post tunnel and Kinney tried to make himself comfortable on the damp floor. Unable to stand and awkward to sit upright he wriggled into a prone position so his ear was against the clay wall and he could see the canary, which to all miners was known as friend. He picked up his wooden stake and pushed it into the clay wall. Clamping his teeth onto the exposed end as he listened, with his teeth.

The silent minutes crept by like hours as Kinney lay back looking at nothing. He looked up at the ceiling that he could not see in this dark hole, so he thought there was nothing to see anyway, unless he put his chin on his chest and looked between his feet to see the dim light from the candle further down the tunnel. He fumbled inside his tunic searching for his pipe. He found it and shook the dottle from the bowl and blew down it to clear it. He did not charge it with fresh baccy, he just liked to suck on it and imagine the taste and aromatic smells of various tobaccos he loved, simply to occupy his mind. He knew the canary was there but he could not really see it. He could touch the cage and poke his finger to disturb the bird, ensuring it was still alive, but... what the feck's that?

His eyes bulged with the terror inflicted upon him by the sound of a single scratch. Is that you Jerry he thought as he removed the pipe and clamped his teeth around the wooden stake protruding from the clay wall? Rigid with fear and near panic he silently reprimanded himself. Ye feckin' Scots worm, listen, feckin' listen. Tha's feckin' crazy to volunteer for this feckin'... what's that? What the feck is that, he thought, as his world began to spin with the puzzle of the mysterious scratch? There it is again. I'm not feckin' dreaming. But wait, feckin' wait. I canne go runnin' to Johnny wi' feck all. Putting his ear to the wooden stake he cringed with doubt and uncertainty. He bit it to feel any trembles. In a flash he was on all fours with his ear jammed against the clay wall. Feck it, I'm off.

Forgetting the canary he moved silently and crawled along the tunnel. Inbuilt discipline prevented him from scrambling like a madman to sound the alarm, which of course he knew had to be whispered to Johnny. He crawled out of the listening tunnel into the main gallery, stood to his full height and stretched his limbs and thought. Which feckin' way is it? When suddenly out of the murkiness came a loaded trolley being pushed by a Chinese coolie.

Stepping aside for the trolley he then scampered into the poorly lit tunnel from whence the trolley had come.

He found Johnny at WO2 Connor's shed, undoing a box, which had a metal plate, inscribed Geophone[12] on the lid.

"What the fuck are ye doing here?" Johnny rasped at Kinney.

"I heard a scratchin' noise in yon feckin' tunnel, so that's what the feck I'm doin' here," whispered Kinney.

WO2 Connor stepped out of the shed.

"Have you got that workin' yet?"

"I'm just about to put it to the test. Kinney 'ere, reckons there's scratching in 't listening tunnel."

"Oh, piss in the King's bedpan! You'd better be fuckin' imaginin' things," implied WO2 Connor, "better that than fuckin' Jerry pokin' his fuckin' nose in."

Johnny fitted the earpieces onto his head and set up the sound sensors so that he could test the sound in each ear. He quickly read the instruction sheet and whipped the earpieces off and put the bits back in the wooden case.

"C'mon, let's go."

At the listening tunnel entrance Johnny realised he could not take the box with him because ingress was on hands and knees. He fitted the headset on and put the sensors in his tunic pockets.

"Bring the torch and the instruction sheet with you," he whispered to Kinney.

Crawling along soundlessly he approached the end of the tunnel. He nearly jumped out of his skin when the canary fluttered right near his head. With great mental effort he stopped himself from kicking Kinney's head with a kneeling back-kick. Kinney also heard the fluttering canary, which sent him into the most utterly depressing cringe.

"I forgot that wee fecker," he whispered, "sorry."

---

[12] geophone - an electronic receiver designed to pick up seismic vibrations on or below the Earth's surface and to convert them into electric impulses

Johnny deftly fitted together the apparatus in the light of the torch as he read the instructions. With the earpieces on his ears and the sensors in each hand he moved them about very slowly. He pulled out a compass and took a reading, then turning to Kinney he whispered.

"Remember two hundred and ninety-five degrees. Now fuck off and take the geophone back to Jim Connor while I get your fuckin' canary."

Silently Kinney moved off with the bits and pieces to put back in the box and walk back to the shed. Johnny sat in the numbness of this awful pit wondering why this claustrophobic nightmare did not seem to have any noticeable effect on his men. Knowing that it did have an effect only enhanced the respect he held for each of them.

Lying alone with his thoughts he allowed them to wander back to the balmy summertime fields of Lancashire where he walked arm in arm with Jinny as they strolled along the footpaths and country lanes surrounded by hedgerows and wild flowers. He loved his country and the place in which he lived, spending the daylight hours in the invigorating fresh air of the countryside, which was his panacea, particularly as most of his life was spent underground at the coalface. The vision of his favourite tree, the great oak in Owl's Wood, filled his mind with ecstatic memories of kissing and loving Jinny within the magical aura of that great tree.

These visions of nature collapsed in a kaleidoscope of colour fading to darkness as a subterranean thump in the clay, not as far away as he initially thought, abruptly ended the daydream. Carefully lifting the canary from the ledge he started to crawl away from the clay face but stopped to listen. Silence, deathly silence filled the potential tomb. A nearby candle reflected in the eyes of the face that looked like it had been hewn out of the clay. The eyes blinked when he heard another distant thump. That is it, that is Jerry placing explosives.

Moments later he was back at the shed with Jim Connor, poring over a chart on the table. Using drawing pins and twine they adjusted the twine from the pin at the listening tunnel on the chart to point two hundred and ninety-five degrees across the chart.

"It depends how far away they are and if they are aware of our presence here, which I don't think they are," said WO2 Connor. "We need Hellfire Jack here to use the geophone because he's an expert and will tell us exactly where Jerry is. Thee make a brew while I send for him."

Hellfire Jack arrived just in time for the brew but he was too concerned with Jerry to be bothered with a cup of tea. Following the line of the twine to the drawing pin he looked at Johnny.

"You used the geophone to get this angle, Sgt Gordon. Why didn't you find the distance?"

"It's the first time I've used it," replied Johnny. "I'm a fuckin' coal miner, not a fuckin' scientist."

"That is where you are wrong, Sergeant. You are a sapper sergeant in the Royal Engineers and you will become a subterranean scientist tout de suite. Now get the geophone and I will show you how to find Jerry," ordered Hellfire Jack.

At the entrance to the listening tunnel, Johnny unpacked the geophone from its box and assembled the stethoscope earpieces and the sound sensors. Hellfire Jack took off his hat and demonstrated the geophone to Johnny and Jim Connor using a compass.

"That's exactly what I did in there," said Johnny, as he pointed down the tunnel.

"Jolly good, Sergeant. Now, for finding the distance you unplug one of the sensors and use both tubes of the stethoscope in one sensor and guess how far away the sound is. This takes time and effort to become an expert guesser, but for now I will be the guesser and you will learn from me. Let's go."

Silently they reached the end of the listening tunnel and both men crouched, their heads touching in the confined space where men changed shifts. With a torch Hellfire Jack donned the headgear and plugged into the sensors. After just a few seconds of moving the sensors without looking at the compass Jack pointed in the direction of the enemy. Johnny looked down at the compass and saw that it

50

was two hundred and ninety-five degrees. They both nodded in agreement. Jack unplugged a sensor and plugged it into the other sensor and listened. He took off the headset and handed it to Johnny who put it on and listened. He could now hear more than one sound but the loudest sound was from the direction of the enemy. Looking puzzled, Johnny took off the headset as Jack whispered to him.

"Jerry is seventy feet away on that bearing. The other noises are our men digging further away in a different direction. Listen again to hear what seventy feet away sounds like. Also, they are much higher than we are and to find them we put the sensors on the wall of the tunnel and find which direction they are in."

Johnny handed back the headset and Jack plugged in the other sensor, put on the headset and placed both sensors on the tunnel wall to find the angle at which the enemy was working. Jack used a protractor to find the angle showing Johnny how to do this.

Back at the shed they huddled over the chart and pinpointed the enemy position.

"If they know we're here they would be above us rather than be there," said Jim Connor, pointing at the twine.

"They don't know we are here," said Hellfire Jack.

Johnny joined in.

"How the hell do you know that? Jerry might have one of these," he pointed to the geophone, "or something similar?"

"Jerry does not know we are here and he has not got one of these, which now you are going to practise with. Get two of your sappers and play with that until you can hear a trench rat pissing in a cook's dixie a hundred feet away," said Hellfire Jack.

"What about Jerry, sir?' asked Johnny, as he pointed at the chart.

"I have hundreds of soldiers digging tunnels all along this Western Front, Sgt Gordon, I will find somebody to take care of Jerry. Meanwhile, you must become an expert listener and so must your men. Try listening to your own men from adjacent galleries. Warrant Officer Connor will show you where to go." Looking at Jim Connor he added, "Is that fine with you, Q?"

51

"Very good, sir. Expert listeners coming up, sir," said Jim Connor.

With that Hellfire Jack saluted and marched off to the main shaft. He climbed the ninety feet to the trenches of the front line where death lingered over every parapet and sandbag. Meanwhile Johnny Gordon and Jim Connor sat with a brew of tea and a box of French biscuits and talked about home.

It was only a matter of time before Johnny and his men became very adept at using the geophone, which was extremely fortunate for them and most unfortunate for the Germans because they had no such apparatus for listening to subterranean earthworks. This secret was kept until after the war was over, so the Germans very quickly became second best at underground warfare.

Nevertheless, they succeeded in killing many miners whose names appeared on the dead and wounded lists printed in the newspapers and the names of men lost to the war were displayed in the entrances to many coalmines. Wives and families of miners dreaded the lists of names arriving only too often with such heartbreaking news. Coal miners were also affected by the loss of workmates in the trenches and tunnels, causing great sadness and anger.

One man, Albert Jennings, could not have cared less.

CHAPTER FOUR

Young Albert Jennings thought all his Christmases had arrived with the departure of Brummie. When Brummie went off to war there was no longer any loitering, awaiting the flapping rug from Ruth in the bedroom. He could now let himself into Ruth's house any evening he liked. At first he was arriving on the doorstep every night but that situation eased somewhat when he found himself in demand from other pretty lonely housewives whose menfolk were on the Western Front fighting for King and country.

He was not a budding gigolo; he did not have the skills or the temperament. He was simply a wayfaring cock, dipping his wick amongst the local wives he thought pretty enough to deserve his large penis and its premature ejaculations. The men at the coalface soon came to know his reputation, so a visit to the pub was often followed by a visit to the dentist or doctor to fix teeth and testicles. His job as a clerk also became uncertain because of the need for men at the coalface. One morning he arrived in the office to find a young lady at his desk and the chief clerk instructing her about the job. He told young Albert to find a large helmet to fit his large head - his muscles were needed more than his pen pushing.

He still visited his bevy of young ladies but his demeanour soon changed and he became uncouth. Ruth was beneath him in bed as he plunged into her and fired his seed and shouted.

"That's for thee, Brummie. I've got thy pick and thy slut."

He needed several stitches in a head wound caused by the po breaking on it. Ruth continued stabbing him with the broken po handle right through the front door and into the street, his trousers for a bandage around his head. Blood everywhere. Little did he know then but young Albert would soon be heading for the Western Front to join unsuspecting cuckolded miners.

Just a few streets away, Beryl, Solly's wife, was sipping a glass of sherry whilst reading a book at the table. The gas mantle was lit on a low light but she liked to have a lit candle at her elbow to lighten the pages and make the book feel more alive as she read.

The coal fire in the large range was flickering, dramatically casting shadows and light into the corners of the room, adding more drama to the story she was reading, a Sapphic[13] tale about high-class French prostitutes who hated men but loved each other. Seemingly the adventures amongst themselves were far more interesting to Beryl than the antics with their male clients.

The coal fire kept the room quite warm, consequently, Beryl was always scantily clad with a skimpy silk bodice that uplifted her breasts making them look larger than they actually were and a lace petticoat she had slit and stitched to expose her leg nearly up to her thigh; thinking it looked oriental and risqué, which it did. Solly loved her prancing around the house in exotic underwear when he was there, but he was in a different hole somewhere in France just now and this cavorting French lady had dismissed him from her mind with the help of a glass or two of Amontillado.

The passage she was reading described the ecstasies of two French ladies, as their lovemaking became more engrossing with their tenderness in kissing and lightly stroking each other's erogenous body parts; even the lace and silk garments seemed to be part of the ritual as their fingers gently caressed their silk covered pubic bones. Her right hand started to wander like it was coming out in sympathy with the French girls' hands. She was in fact copying them as her hand first went to her bosom and found her nipples hardening to her touch, just like when Solly did it – but Solly was not there. Her fingers slid down the lace and found the slit but pulled her hand back and rounded her mons pubis, caressing and lightly squeezing it, the silk enhanced the sensations that spread across her belly. With a hint of self-consciousness her fingers slid

---

13 Sapphic tale - of or relating to the Greek poet Sappho

across the garment and again found the oriental slit but this time her fingers ventured in and found her wet labia, which banished any shred of self-consciousness as her fingers closed on her clitoris.

Holding the book flat on the table with one hand as the other played naturally with her fanny, the words were taking her to greater sensations and when she turned the page there was an exquisite drawing of the two French girls, one of them with her tongue licking the other's clitoris. Her orgasm rushed at her as she cried in ecstasy and she felt as though her ovaries were gushing into her vagina. She was very wet. Her orgasm subsided, leaving her gasping and greedy for another but when she touched herself the sensitivity shock was so great, she had to wait for that little body part to recover. So she waited.

Later, in bed, she wondered what it would be like with another woman, thinking that it was not adultery, was it? No that is with a man, but whom do I like? The lovely Cathryn came to mind and she thought I will lend Cathryn the book and see where it takes us.

Further down the street on the opposite side, Jinny was in bed holding her belly waiting for the little kick that told her a little man was trying to come out. She was truly miserable because the war had ruined the chances of getting the house she wanted in Kent Street. She wore Johnny's long nightshirt and had not washed it since he left to go to war so it still had his scent on it. Nor had she washed Johnny's pillowcase. She held that in a cuddle between the bump and her face.

Thoughts of Johnny flashed through her mind constantly; even her dreams were of Johnny, she was thinking about him now. Her heart-breaking loneliness was crushing her robust character and being pregnant was not helping. Even Ma, her mother, was worried about her; but Ma's thoughts were of Billy her only son. The words please Great Lord of the universe keep my boy safe, glory be to you Great Father, often escaped her lips.

The first thing Jinny did every morning was walk to the colliery to check the death list at the gates. Lists were not pinned up every day, only when casualties were reported, which were too often anyway. Old lists were removed after a week so when a new list went up it could be seen from a distance and Jinny would hold her belly and run like hell to see who was on it. Gasping for breath she would frantically read the list, which of course may only have one or two names on it, then slouch off home feeling sorry for the families of the fallen and relieved for not seeing Johnny on the list.

She dreaded seeing the postman or the telegraph boy because the postman delivered the form, 'It is my painful duty to inform you', or the telegram, 'Regret to inform you'. She wondered why sometimes the names appeared on the list at the gates before the postman arrived with the dreaded form. What the hell, they're dead anyway!

The energy of her thoughts dissipated as sleep approached. One final thought was that she would write to Johnny tomorrow but still not tell him about the expected baby until it arrived and was in good health, then I'll tell him - but she dreamt about tunnels and men digging like moles.

*

The proliferation of tunnels along the Western Front meant, of course, that many more miners were needed to complement the hard-stretched sappers who were often taken from a tunnel to another of more tactical importance. Such was the fate of Johnny Gordon and his men who had worked in several tunnels and now they were going back to an area known as The Glory Hole.

"These tunnels have been 'ere for years," said Tommy Tudor.

"Aye, the locals dug 'em to hide their cattle, and 'emselves,' replied Andy Emans, as he dumped his kit on the hard chalk floor, "Jerry'll need bigger artillery shells to reach us in 'ere," he added.

"He'll come at us from below once he knows we're 'ere, an' ye can bet 'e feckin' knows we'se 'ere awready," chirped McKinney.

"Why don't ye eat thy fuckin' sporran instead of spouting shite all fuckin' day?" said Yiggs Bliss, placing his kit next to Andy's.

The men gathered round as Johnny returned from his briefing with the Commanding Officer.

"Ye all know about The Glory Hole, we've been here before. It should be called The Shit Hole because that's what it is. This 'ere is Inch Street and it goes all t' way round t' Tay Street, that away," he said as he pointed along the tunnel. "This 'ere is a repair job an' Jerry is busy diggin' under Sausage Valley, which is along 'ere," he stooped to look along the black hole leading away to the North. "We use our bayonets to cut ledges for candles and any diggin' as needs doin' an' we wear clean sandbags on our feet, so leave boots 'ere just inside t' tunnel."

He took his boots off and wrapped a sandbag around each foot. The men quickly and silently did the same. He drew his pistol and indicated that Taff do likewise.

"Ye all know the drill. Me 'n Taff do the recce an' you follow, placin' candles."

Johnny and Taff crept cautiously along the tunnel using their torches, one shining along the roof of the tunnel the other along the floor seeking out tripwires in case the enemy had discovered the tunnel and laid booby-traps. The foul air and a wet floor along with the numbing silence compounded the tense situation with each careful step as they approached the end of the tunnel, which was a chalk face with embedded slivers and chunks of flint. The two men hunkered down to listen. Taff pulled out a wooden stake and slowly pushed it into the chalk face and bit on it. Stillness for a moment, then Taff showed three fingers and pointed at an angle slightly above them. Johnny indicated to get out.

On their way out they met the rest of the men bagging debris and passing it back to the exit that could be seen in the flickering candles illuminating this part of the tunnel. Johnny ushered everyone out into Inch Street. The men stood there in silent awe waiting to know what would happen next.

Johnny whispered in Brummie's ear.

"Get the geophone and tell Jim Connor that Jerry is very near and we need to blow him before he blows us." Looking at Solly, Andy, Allballs and Yiggs, he indicated for them to go with Brummie and whispered to Solly, "Get two camouflets from Jim Connor."

As a result of so many earthworks by the sappers on both sides, discovery and breakthrough into each other's tunnels often happened. So in readiness for this a pre-prepared charge called a camouflet was always ready for use when this happened.

Johnny ordered the remaining men to continue illuminating the tunnel while he and Taff crept forward again to the face. Both of them were on all fours, listening intently. The other sappers were silently working toward them and Billy Nolan was first to reach Johnny.

"The geophone is waitin' for thee," whispered Billy, jerking his thumb over his shoulder.

"Pass it on and get out. Tell Solly to prepare the charges ready for placing," whispered Johnny.

Billy crept back to form the human chain needed to silently pass the geophone to Johnny and Taff. Donning the earphones and plugging in the sensors Johnny immediately reacted to the sounds in his ears from the sensors. He stiffened, alarmed. He grabbed Taff's collar and pulled him to whisper in his ear.

"They're behind us, back there," he pointed back along the tunnel, "get the men out now, quietly," whispered Johnny.

Taff crawled back towards the men indicating to get out. They knew the drill and about turned on all fours and silently crawled toward Inch Street. Johnny continued with the geophone trying to locate the direction of travel of the German tunnel, which was criss-crossing above him headed for the British Front Line.

Suddenly the roof collapsed, burying Taff and a body fell in on top of him shouting and screaming in German. In the chaos of the moment Johnny shot the German and scrambled up over the rubble to shoot at figures he could see in the German tunnel. Four German miners were killed and an officer lay wounded but Johnny was unaware because he was too busy using a German shovel digging like a maniac to free Taff from under a ton of earth.

On the other side of the fall-in the sappers were digging with bare hands, pulling clumps of earth out of the way. They heard the sound of gunfire and guessed it was Johnny or Taff doing the shooting.

Johnny found Taff's foot and pulled off the sandbag to find a pulse. It was there. He pulled away more earth and luckily found Taff's pistol because he heard German voices approaching along their tunnel. He climbed up into the German tunnel half in half out and aimed both pistols in the direction of the voices, and when they loomed into view he fired and killed more Germans. He felt the rubble beneath his feet move as his men retrieved Taff by yanking him out from under him. A hand appeared with a grenade in it. Johnny grabbed it and pulled the pin. Holding it briefly, while trying to see along the tunnel, he threw it and ducked down to avoid the blast and shrapnel. The blast deafened him for a moment but the adrenaline kept him alert and bristling for a fight. He felt a movement behind him and up came Allballs and Brummie with grenades.

"Fuckin' hell, tha's kilt 'em all," said Allballs.

"Not all," replied the wounded officer who lay ten feet away in the tunnel. "I am shot in the shoulder and thigh and if you don't rescue me I will bleed to death in this French hole," the German officer spoke perfect English with a patrician accent. "Take me to your Empire Jack please. It will be an honour to meet him."

Like ferrets, the men raced across to him and established the wounds before dragging him back and passing him down to the others. Johnny took his fancy pistol, which was still holstered.

"Ye means Hellfire Jack don't ye?"

"Your newspapers call him Empire Jack but Hellfire Jack sounds better."

"You'll savvy when you meet him," Johnny chuckled.

"I will tell him how brave you are."

Johnny scowled mockingly.

"I shoulda' killed you."

"You reap what you sow, Sergeant, remember that."

Jim Connor arrived with men pulling trolleys loaded with explosives.

"Right then. Get this lot into Jerry's tunnel and... who the fuck's that?" he exclaimed, when he recognised the German officer as the enemy.

"He's Kaiser Bill's bum boy," said Johnny, "he's too posh to be anything else.'

"Right-o boys, get 'im on t' trolley an' up to HQ," ordered Jim Connor.

"I think a doctor is needed before I run out of blood. Please, I'm sure your Hellfire Jack has no need for a dead German engineer officer," pleaded the German.

Jim Connor glared at Johnny.

"Why is this fucker still alive? You normally kill every fucker. He'll be askin' for a fuckin' surgeon an' a glass of Schnapps next. Fuckin' gerrim o'er t' medics."

The German grimaced with pain as the men moved him.

"Please, Quartermaster, I am seriously wounded and I need..."

"How the fuck does thee know I'm the quartermaster?" roared Jim Connor.

"That badge on your sleeve and I heard one of the men call you Q so nothing sinister about that, Q."

"Move! Fuckin' shift 'im outta here afore I shoots 'im myself," snarled Jim Connor. "Now get that fuckin' tunnel prepared for t' blow."

Now that the element of surprise had gone the men quickly put their boots back on and started charging the tunnel with explosives. Taff was none the worse for his ordeal and joined Johnny to recce the German tunnel. They climbed up into the German tunnel as the sappers passed the explosives along to the face beneath it. No sounds were made because the rigid discipline required tactical silence to do anything, even after shots were fired. Carefully stepping over the dead miners they moved forward with torches along the murky tunnel. They both had pistols and grenades at the ready as they crept along then rounded a bend and saw two more tunnels branching off the main tunnel.

"These are old workings," whispered Johnny, "built for troop movement under no man's land. That officer and his men must have been surveying to see how far to dig to reach our front lines."

"Or maybe planning to blow a crater right under our front line," added Taff. "That mine of Jim Connor's ain't enough to collapse this lot. We need a big bang along 'ere. Get thee back an' tell Jim Connor we need guns 'n grenades along 'ere an' a ton o' ammonal[14]."

Taff was uncertain and troubled and was left alone thinking as Johnny crept forward toward the two tunnels.

"Pssst!" Taff hissed.

Johnny turned and stage whispered.

"Fuck off!" then continued on his way.

Taff hurriedly crept away to inform Jim Connor about the two tunnels.

Johnny reached the Y junction and lay prone so he could see or hear any movement from either tunnel whilst presenting a smaller target of himself should shooting begin. Easing two grenades out of his pouches he placed them to his front ready to throw if need be. He lay there in total silence and a blackness that lesser men could not endure. Claustrophobia was the devil Johnny conquered years ago at the coalface of Bold Colliery, but danger presented itself in different guises down this pit and Johnny expected it to arrive any time now.

A flicker of light behind him made him turn his head to see the approach of Taff and others, but as they loomed into sight a sudden knock and hiss of a German stick grenade landed right next to him made him snatch it and toss it back into the blackness whence it came.

"Grenade!" he shouted and buried his head into his arms to protect his face.

---

[14] ammonal – a high explosive mixture of 3 parts of ammonium nitrate and 1 part of aluminium

The grenade exploded, killing several Germans just thirty feet away from him. He immediately yanked out the pins on his two grenades and waited three seconds before tossing them along the tunnel. He knew the grenades were on five-second fuses and he did not want them coming back at him. Taff and the sappers opened up with small arms fire as Johnny rolled to his left out of the line of fire. The fire fight provided flashing light so he could see along the other tunnel, which was clear up to where it changed direction about forty feet away and headed west. Johnny thought that if his bearings were correct that tunnel ran parallel to the British front line and could have tunnels branching off to place mines under the front line. It must be investigated.

The firefight died away to sporadic firing and after a few more grenades were thrown along the tunnel, silence. Solly and Tat (Tommy Tudor) advanced to investigate and found several dead Germans and heard others actually running away along the tunnel. After checking each body, ensuring they were all dead, Solly crept along the tunnel following the runners.

"Where the fuck is ye headed?" asked Tat.

"As far along 'ere as I can. We can't just fuckin' leave wi' out knowin' where it's fuckin' leadin' to."

"Oh, yes we fuckin' can. Look how wide it is; a fuckin' regiment could march through 'ere. I've seen enough to know what this is. It's an advance route fo' t' Jerry."

"Aye," said Solly, "that's why we gotta see what's up yonder."

Johnny suddenly appeared.

"Where the fuck is thee goin' Solly?"

"T' see where it…"

"Its goin' to fuckin' Liverpool, where your headstone will be waitin' for thee. Get fuckin' back 'ere an' tell Jim Connor we needs a machine gunner down 'ere fast!"

Solly slunk back and handed Tat a couple of grenades.

"Cop for these, in case Jerry comes around t' bend," Solly growled.

Johnny beckoned Taff and whispered.

62

"I'm takin' Allballs, Kinney an' Brummie to recce this other tunnel. Tha knows t' drill, get t' geophone and listen for Jerry above, I don't want 'im blowin' this lot down on us."

Taff immediately beckoned Allballs, Kinney and Brummie and whispered.

"Go with Johnny."

They crept over to Johnny as the others, Yiggs, Andy, Billy and Tat, prepared defensive positions in the tunnel and waited for Solly to arrive with a machine gunner. Johnny and his men moved tactically along the tunnel and crept cautiously around the bend and out of sight of Taff and the others. After just a few yards Johnny discovered a much smaller tunnel cut into the wall to his left. He beckoned Kinney and whispered.

"Get along there an' see if Jerry's planted explosives. We'll wait here for thee."

Into the black hole Kinney crawled on all fours. Once he had crawled two yards inside he switched on his torch and moved on. His mind was swimming with claustrophobia as he ventured forward through the tunnel and over small clumps of earth where parts of the roof had collapsed - a nightmare that ordinary men could not endure. With emotions crushing his every move he stoically kept closed the floodgates of panic as he crawled into a large chamber loaded with explosives. Frantically scratching around searching for the initiation set, which detonates the explosives, he discovered an electric cable buried beneath him. Following the cable by pulling it from beneath the packed earth it disappeared into the boxes of explosives. He shone his torch between the ends of the boxes and found the initiation set right in the centre of the charge. Crafty Kinney decided not to pull it in case it was booby-trapped, he about turned and crawled back along the tunnel lifting the cable out of the ground as he went.

Reaching Johnny he crawled out and pulled up the cable that Johnny was practically standing on. Out of the ground popped the end of the cable with two copper ends pared for connecting, to what? Johnny knew immediately.

"A fuckin' ring main for a multiple explosion. That's what that fuckin' dandy officer was up to, connecting charges to a fuckin' ring main," said Johnny. He grabbed Brummie and said, "Run back an' tell Taff to go to where we got the officer and tell 'im to look for t' ring main." He glared at Kinney and Allballs, "Let's see what else there is. Find t' other fuckin' tunnels an' we'll find t' fuckin' cables."

Along the gallery from where the cable was discovered, Johnny and his men found more charges and neutralised all of them. He instructed Taff and his men to dismantle each charge and bring all of the explosives back to where the machine gunner and an infantry grenade team were waiting for Jerry to show his face while Johnny went to report to Jim Connor.

Jim Connor accompanied Johnny to HQ and arranged for him to report directly to Hellfire Jack, who was entertaining the captured German officer now recovering from his dressed and treated wounds. The German put down his glass of wine and grinned as the two men entered the office and announced.

"Ah, here comes my brave captor. You should be proud of him, Colonel."

Jim Connor and Johnny stood to attention as the Chief Clerk announced.

"Sergeant Gordon reporting. Sir!"

The Chief Clerk marched out and closed the door.

Hellfire Jack lurched out of his chair and glared at Johnny.

"This is mighty unusual leaving your men down the hole to speak to me, Sergeant Gordon. It had better be important."

"It is! Sir! Speak, Sergeant Gordon," Jim Connor snapped.

Johnny looked the German in the eye with so much hate it could be felt.

"I should have killed you," he said, in a voice unlike Hellfire Jack had ever heard the likes of before. "I found all of your attack tunnels and removed tons of your explosives, which I will now use under your front line, you Jerry bastard." Johnny looked at Hellfire Jack, "He was connecting charges to a ring main for multiple charges, all along this section of the front line, sir, which tells me Jerry is about to attack."

"What?" Hellfire Jack spluttered and turning to the now white-faced German he said, "Get out!"

"I'll take care of the prisoner, sir. I think you'd best go with Sergeant Gordon to see what he's found," Jim Connor said, drawing his pistol.

Hellfire Jack and Johnny rushed out of the HQ bunker on their way to the tunnel, as Jim Connor escorted the German to the Field Ambulance area where the dead and dying were laid out in neat rows. He pointed to an empty stretcher, next to a wounded soldier and as the German lay down Jim Connor blew his brains out and instructed a nearby medic.

"Throw him to the rats, an' if any fucker asks, he was escaping."

CHAPTER FIVE

The hazy days of midsummer heralded the coming of thousands of allied troops in readiness for the beginning of the Battle of the Somme - July 1st, 1916, the darkest day in British military history, was the first day of the battle, which took 1.3 million casualties during its one hundred and forty-one days duration.

Royal Engineers Sergeant Johnny Gordon and his section of sappers were sent to an infantry battalion to assist in the advance across no man's land. His duties included the use of explosives to clear collapsed tunnels and trenches and to repair captured dugouts for the advancing infantry to use.

This first day of the battle was also the darkest for Sergeant Johnny Gordon because his best pal, Corporal Taff Dupree, was badly wounded by a sniper with a shot to the head. This type of wound was called a Blighty because the wounded soldier needed to be treated back in England. With a broken heart Johnny said farewell to Taff and the others waved a sad goodbye as the ambulance took him away.

Sgt Gordon and his men Lance Corporal 'Solly' Salisbury and sappers Billy Nolan, 'Kinney' McKinney, 'Brummie' Howell, 'Allballs' Alcock, 'Yiggs' Barry Bliss, 'Tat' Tommy Tudor and 'Andy' Emans were all veterans, having been in action for many months and had become desensitised to death and destruction, which is the bone of contention between experienced warriors and inexperienced upper-class junior officers.

And so the battle started. Johnny and his men supported The King's Liverpool Regiment in their attack on the enemy held Trones Wood area. The night was bright with exploding star shells illuminating anything that moved in no man's land. Johnny's eyes were saucer-like, bright as an owl's, peering from beneath the steel rim of his helmet. The flash of an exploding shell exposed the terror in his bright eyes as mud and debris rained down on him. Then an arm and shoulder attached to a head landed with a thud right in front of Johnny. He stared at the head of his brother-in-law, Billy Nolan, looking sightlessly back at him.

"Hello, Billy, I'll write to Ma and Jinny if I get out alive. If."

Looking as if his face was cast in bronze, with bits of clay sticking to it and his tunic, the brooding eyes now darkened under the rim of his helmet as he scanned the broken ground in front of the trench. In the silence of the moment a snarl creased his dirty face. A large rat and then another tried to drag the severed arm away to their hidden nest. No doubt they have young to feed. There's plenty of raw meat around here. As if in slow motion the barrel of a Webley pistol appeared alongside his right eye. Ever so cautiously it lined up on Billy's remains. His eyes glittered with rage as he fired. He dropped to his knee on the fire step as the parapet of sandbags disintegrated under withering machine-gun and sniper fire from the ever-watching enemy.

"Fuckin' 'ell!" he shouted, "So much for softening up afore we goes o'er top. Our long-range snipers are dropping short. That was Billy Nolan blown to bits!' He crossed himself, "Great Lord, take Billy to life everlasting. Amen."

He thought of Ma and Jinny's sadness when they got the telegram informing them of his death. Bloody hell.

Dirty faces appeared in the darkness like ghostly apparitions. They had been there all the time, waiting, waiting for the dreaded whistle that would send them all to Hell. Johnny looked at the expression of absolute trust in the faces of his men. Warriors. Brummie shifted his weight to his other leg nudging Allballs. The regional accents of these men were sometimes difficult to understand, nevertheless a joy to hear the rich English words of the early twentieth century above the noise of an artillery barrage.

"Fuck off, Brummie, lean on some fucker else. Hey, Sarge, can thee get t' artillery to kill t' fuckin' Bosch instead of us?"

Johnny poked Andy with his pistol.

"Go tell the signaller to tell the drop shorts to put their fuckin' shells into the trees to our front."

"Okay, Sarge, but what about the officers?" asked Andy.

"Don't fuckin' tell 'em, just tell the fuckin' sigs man I said. Now fuck off an' keep yer fuckin' 'ead down." He nodded at Allballs, "Ye go wi' 'm, one of ye should get through."

The two sappers disappeared along the trench as more shells rained down on no man's land right in front of their trench, creating a tangible disrupting energy felt by the men through the earth and in the air. Loose items flapped and careened into the sky as grim faces pressed into the trench wall. The maelstrom flung dead men high and stinking human remains fell into the trench and onto the men - a daily occurrence. Solly heaved a leg out of the trench and grabbed a helmeted bloody head, ripping off the fancy spiked German helmet.

"At last! Got me fuckin' souvenir an' didn't have to shoot the bastard to get it. Fuck off, Fritz," he roared.

The rotting head sailed over the top into no man's land as Brummie coughed his guts out.

"That head must've been there for over a week, there wasn't any skin on it. My nasal hair has fell out with the fuckin' stink."

In the darkness Kinney's deep Scotch voice boomed along the trench.

"Aye, an' ye'd best chuck the other bits oot afore the feckin' flies congregate on us. Feckin' dysentery an' aw' kindsa shit diseases are…"

"Up yer fuckin' kilt, Kinney," shouted Brummie, "it's bad enough wi' the fuckin' Bosch an' rats wi' out you witterin' on about fuckin' flies."

Andy and Allballs moved fast along the trench looking for the signaller. They stopped momentarily to ask an infantry corporal for directions.

"Fifty yards further on and ye'll see a tiny blue and white flag at the entrance to his dugout," said the corporal.

On they went scrambling passed crouching infantrymen who added to the various obstacles in their path. Finding the signaller they were surprised to see he was a lance corporal in the Royal

68

Engineers. The lance corporal looked up from his little table as he was shouting into a field telephone. Placing the handset in its cradle he grinned at the two sappers.

"Nice day for it then, chaps. What the fuck are you doing here?" he asked.

"Tryin' ta stay alive," said Andy. "We'se gettin' killed by our own artillery an' our sergeant told us ta tell ye ta tell artillery long-range snipers to get shells into yon trees eighty yards in front of our position."

The lance corporal pulled a grubby sheet of paper onto the table.

"Show me where you are on here," he asked.

Andy could see the zigzag line of the trench system and recognised exactly where their position was on the rough drawing.

"Right there," he said, pointing with his bayonet.

"Right, by the time you get back you'll hear an incoming cluster. If you're not back here one minute later I'll tell the barrage boys to continue. Savvy?"

"Savvy," said Andy, and off they went racing back to Johnny and the others.

They were just in time for the momentary ceasefire, a lull in the barrage, a moment of silence.

"If that dopey fuckin' officer blows 'is whistle now, we all die," Johnny muttered. "The fuckin' krauts will hear it an' cut us to fuckin' pieces."

The silence hurt with ears ringing from the previous barrage. Faces pressed against the trench walls moved and were etched with acute trepidation. Eyes glittered with alarm as Johnny looked along the trench, taut eyes strained.

"Where the fuck is those two fuckers? They should be back by now. The fuckin' sigs man is along the trench, not in fuckin' Paris."

"They musta got through to the sigs bloke, Sarge. I bet they're resighting the guns into the woods yonder. And here they are!" Brummie piped up.

The silence was broken by the overhead whining of incoming artillery shells and the ground shook with the impacting explosives. Johnny looked cautiously over the top.

"Gimme your fuckin' tin hat, Brummie."

Brummie passed his helmet with his bayonet to Johnny who cautiously raised it above the parapet for the snipers to shoot at. As though death had lost all meaning he snatched a quick look across no man's land at the German positions. Nothing, apart from indescribable noise as the trees hiding the Germans were blasted with high explosive and shrapnel shells. Johnny grinned at his men.

"Thank fuck for that. Trones Wood will be firewood by t' morning." Looking at the panting Andy and Allballs, "Bloody good job, ye two. Sigs bloke is on t' ball too."

"Aye, Sarge, an' 'es a bloody sapper lance corporal," said Allballs.

"That explains it then, don't it, lad. Sapper initiative and skills," said Johnny, "not like this fuckin' clown," he added, pointing along the trench.

A figure loomed up out of the murky cordite fumes wearing an officer's peaked cap of the King's Liverpool Regiment. The men started to stand up to attention for Captain David Davidson, aged about twenty-five and known as Daffy behind his back.

"As you were, men. Stay down," he said.

As Johnny stepped down from the trench firing step[15] to eyeball the officer it was evident there was no love lost between them. Johnny's fatalistic instincts blossomed when around young upper class officers still searching for leadership qualities they would never achieve.

"Sergeant Gordon, I know you are Royal Engineers on detachment to me. Which means you obey my orders."

Looking around him at the grim faces of battle-hardened men he wondered if he should lower his tone.

"So why are you so far away from the battalion lines? I risk my damn neck each time I need you," he added.

---

[15] fire step - ledge cut into the trench wall

It seemed like the words hung in the air for a moment. Johnny sighed.

"How many men have you lost in t' barrage, sir?" he asked.

"Too many. Why do you ask?"

"Because I have only lost one man since this battle started last week and he was killed by our own fuckin' artillery five minutes ago. I don't trust our artillery gunners so I keep my men on the left flank, on the fringe of the gunners' barrage, that way we don't suffer from drop shorts. Thee, on t' other hand, sit directly in t' line of fire. Tha's had drop shorts, haven't ye?"

Daffy lifted his hat and wiped grime and sweat from his brow.

"That is why I have come for you. The HQ bunker has been hit and has fallen in, burying men and battalion ammo, which includes your high explosives. So get your men and follow me. Spades are onsite."

Johnny's facial expression was enough to galvanise his men into action - let us show the fucking cannon fodder how the Royal Engineers win fucking wars. Without a word the men had already moved. They travelled surprisingly fast in such confined spaces, so Daffy was left to keep up at the rear. The terrible noise of artillery fire exploding amongst the trees just eighty yards away seemed to spur the men on. They turned the first corner of the captured zigzag designed trench, which traversed in different directions, each traverse being approximately thirty yards long, and jumped over the dead bodies of German soldiers partially covered with the dirt of collapsed trench walls. Corner after stumbling corner took away their breath but there was no slowing down of these hardened warriors.

The trench ran deeper where the HQ area began and the sappers raced past snipers who were standing on fire step cut into the trench wall, the noise of their shooting drowned by the artillery barrage. Up ahead they witnessed the bloody scene of collapsed walls fallen into the dugout, a huge crater of buried men and equipment, body parts everywhere heads, legs, guts and even dead rats.

71

Breathless, the men grabbed spades and picks to join the rescue diggers, some of whom were wounded but digging nonetheless. Johnny looked at his sappers taking to the task of pulling live and dead bodies from the pile of earth. He noticed a small gap where the rubble met the trench wall. The penny dropped.

"Clear the trench. Get out of here!" he shouted.

Daffy the officer grabbed his sleeve and pulled him around.

"What the hell do you think you are doing, Sergeant? Get them digging."

Johnny grabbed Daffy's arm and pulled him forward, yelling.

"See that! See fuckin' that! That is the chamber where the bastards tunnelled. Where the explosives were planted, right under our fuckin' feet. This is not a drop short, it's a fuckin' tunnel mine. There'll be another to kill the rescuers in a minute so move, now. Come on!"

The sappers had already scampered off along the trench, knowing the Germans' barbaric methods of killing, but more soldiers were rushing to help from the other direction, dozens of them.

The earth moved beneath Johnny's feet and his ear drums crackled with the sound of exploding earth and a force behind him sent him headlong into the trench wall five yards away at the traverse. This stunned him for a moment. Then he twisted around to see tons of earth and men hurtling skywards - bodies being torn apart by the energy of the explosion. Heads and limbs separated flew high into the sky, then tons of earth falling to kill and bury more men under what formed the new rim of the crater.

He looked at his feet to see the moving hand of Daffy. He was buried under a ton of earth. Johnny screamed at his men to help him but the scream was not noticed in the stunning silence following the explosion. All ears were deaf just then, but slowly sounds came creeping back into the senses and Taff and the sappers were suddenly there, tearing the earth from Daffy as they dragged him to his feet. Johnny brushed himself down with his hands and emptied soil from his helmet.

"Sit him on t' fire step, he'll be fine in a minute. Leave him, we've a job to do," ordered Johnny, as Daffy quickly recovered.

"What are you going to do?" asked Daffy.

"The same to them."

Johnny shouted to his sappers.

"C'mon, you lot, get those fuckin' explosives, we'll give 'em a fuckin' surprise."

"You're going to open their tunnel?" Daffy asked, perplexed.

"They won't be expecting us at their end. They'll have closed it off because of the back blast," replied Johnny.

"You reap what you sow, Sergeant," said Daffy.

"The last bloke as said that t' me is fuckin' dead. An' you're right, sir. I am the fuckin' reaper. Just watch those Bosch head for t' stars when I light 'em up."

Even though Daffy knew Johnny had just saved his life, his eyes shone with acute hatred, a hatred Johnny knew existed but chose to ignore. Johnny knew from bitter experience that upstart officers all go the same way, a crumpled, bleeding heap in no man's land, the harsh reality of existence on the Western Front.

The sappers dug like the experienced coal miners they all were. The tunnel was soon exposed and the explosives passed down into it, where Johnny expertly made up the initiation sets for the enormous underground bomb. All set and they were ready to move along the tunnel. Johnny led the way shining his torch whilst holding a length of wire to his front to detect trip-wire booby traps, which the Germans often set for the many thousands of young inexperienced soldiers who did not know any better. The sappers followed him in pairs, carrying explosives - ammonal in fifty-pound tins. Bent double because of the height of the tunnel roof, the men sweated profusely as they stumbled along in the darkness. Not a sound did they make because it was certain death if the enemy, who were now being blasted by the British artillery, heard them. Johnny took no chances and led his men cautiously along the narrow tunnel. The impacting shells caused the earth to tremble beneath their feet and it got worse as they neared the German lines. The dull thump of exploding ordnance showed the concern on each hardened face and their eyes glittered with trepidation. They knew, to a man, that one single direct hit could bring down the roof and crush them to death and their eyes betrayed their emotions.

The earth tremored and the noise increased as the ground rose toward the opening shaft where Johnny knew the Germans were sheltering on the other side of the blocked tunnel. Soundlessly the sappers placed their tins of ammonal in a stack in order for the greatest energy release on detonation. In pairs the sappers returned silently whence they came. Into the murky light of the trench they crawled and into the welcoming hands of their corporal. Taff was back.

"Come on boys, I've got a brew on over yere. Hot 'n sweet it be too," he said, with the baritone Welsh accent that was music to the men. "Save some for me and my lovely sergeant or I'll piss in the next brew," he chuckled.

The sappers were delighted with the return of their corporal and relieved to be out of the suffocating tunnel into which Taff now disappeared, to find Johnny creeping toward him uncoiling the electric cable to blow the mine. Johnny grunted appreciatively at the sight of Taff. These men loved each other for what they were, warriors.

"Ye got a Blighty; a fuckin' 'ead wound. What the fuck're ye doin' 'ere?' Ye should be down t' pit diggin' fuckin' coal, ye crazy bastard."

"Now then boyo, have less of the crazy, an' the coal can wait while we kick out the Hun. Besides it was only a twenty stitches job between my temple an' my ear. Look."

Taff raised his helmet and in the poor light Johnny could see the livid fresh scar running around his head.

"Shoulda put a bolt in thy neck. Ye look like Frankenstein's fuckin' monster," Johnny grunted.

"I didn't know ye could read? Now I know where thy sense of humour comes from, fuckin' Mary Shelley's Frankenstein," Taff chuckled.

Greeting ceremony over they got down to killing Germans.

The officer, Daffy, scrambled over the rubble looking a bit nervous as Johnny and Taff cut fuses and assembled explosive primers[16] and detonators for the initiation sets.

"Sergeant Gordon, we go over the top when the barrage ends. Soon."

Johnny looked up from his task straight into Daffy's eyes.

"That's great news, sir. Ye lot go o'er top and we'll go under t' top through there. And I would like to take a grenade team of thy men with me."

Captain Davidson was taken aback and stuttered.

"I - I - I've never done that before. My men? My bloody men? Who do you think you are? You bloody rag-tag bunch of didicoys."

Johnny absorbed the venom staring back without expression. There was no emotion on his face but there was ice in his soul for the inexperienced toffs, responsible for large numbers of casualties, such as this dubious twit. He replied in a measured tone.

"Me an' my men 'ave been in action for a long time, many months 'n kilt 'undreds of Bosch. We've done this many a time. Thee's just started 'ere last week 'n thousands of ye are dead already. So, listen if ye value thy men."

That worked.

"What do you want to do?" asked Daffy, grudgingly.

"When the barrage lifts I will blow the Bosch out of their trench, which is directly opposite us here. They have machine guns aimed right at us an' the moment thee blows that fuckin' whistle they'll start firing. Don't blow t' whistle until my bomb goes off and count to twenty and then blow t' whistle to warn the Hun thee's coming so he can shoot the shit out of ye."

The officer, Daffy, was now even more nervous and angry as Johnny's words made sense in his reluctant mind. He checked his watch.

"My orders are to go over the top when the last shell drops in just over one hour," he said, meaningfully.

---

[16] primer - gun cotton detonator safety fuse

"Twenty seconds ain't goin' to make any odds, but if ye doesn't do as I ask many more of thy men will die. My sappers an' your grenade team will kill the machine gunners afore they kill all of ye. Think about it," said Johnny.

With an acquiescent nod, Daffy scrambled back over the rubble and dead soldiers and was narrowly missed by a sniper's bullet as he unthinkingly looked across no man's land. Kinney commented on the sniper.

"See that, Sarge? They fuckin' snipers are firing wi' shells falling all around 'em, an' I bet that toff blows his fuckin' whistle afore our bomb goes off."

"What do ye expect, Kinney? He's a fuckin' infantry officer; his whistle is more important to him than the men who he thinks are urchins from some shitty Liverpool back street," Solly replied.

Brummie joined the banter.

"If he had a brain, he'd be fuckin' dangerous. We've seen enough arseholes like him to know he won't be around much longer."

"Sithee, if yon's brain was made of gunpowder he wouldn't have enough to blow his fuckin' hat off. See how he holds his head, like he's got shit on his upper lip," Allballs chipped in.

Johnny and Taff smiled as the banter rolled on. Taff gave an order.

"Either make a brew or get some kip."

"Och aye," said Kinney, "yers all talk shite anyway. I'm fer a brew. C'mon, Andy, get the kettle on."

"Get it your feckin' self, I'm 'avin' a kip," replied Andy.

The sappers rested with their backs to the slant of the crater, not quite horizontal but not vertical either. Exposed timbers protruding from the ground and the heap of corpses not yet removed stopped them sliding to the bottom of the crater. Sniper fire had prevented this dreadful task.

The sound of snoring emanated from the crater and, as the noise of the battlefield kept them on their toes, the infantrymen looked on in amazement and watched the sleeping sappers. Sleeping on the hoof was second nature to these men who were by now totally desensitised to the relentless loss of life. The young infantrymen looked on, not yet understanding that to survive the harshest realities of existence on these battlefields it is better to have previously lived a harsh life. If they lacked that core mental strength then chances are they would be lucky to survive. Consistently, in the presence of death and destruction, a cavalier attitude was just another shield against insanity. So with the stoicism of pit ponies the men slept. All except for Johnny who looked over them with shaded eyes. He knew that one shout would get a hair-trigger reaction from his men. Then Captain Davidson arrived in the crater on all fours, his wild eyes glistening with fear.

"Quick as you can, Sergeant Gordon, your Royal Engineer signaller has lost contact. He says the line is broken by artillery shells and must be repaired before the attack."

"He's not my concern, we are not signallers we're miners. I know nowt about signals," growled Johnny.

"You will report immediately with one or two of your sappers to the signals corporal in his dugout. Now! That is a direct order, which you must obey or face the firing squad. Follow me!" shouted Daffy.

Johnny looked at his men and pointed to Kinney and Andy.

"Come on, else we'll not win this fuckin' war." Then looking at his other men he snarled, "No fucker moves from this spot 'til we return, savvy?"

They all nodded affirmatively.

Johnny and his two sappers followed Captain Davidson along the trench to the signaller's dugout where the lance corporal was busy pulling out reels of wire from a metal drum.

"This weighs half a hundredweight so I'm giving you about thirty yards and I'll pare the ends for you and give you the tool to pare the ends of the damaged wire," said the lance corporal.

"I'm a coal miner, what in fuck's name are ye talkin' about?" asked Johnny.

"Repairing the field telephone line, look," he said, holding the wire for Johnny to see, "join the new to the old, like this," he demonstrated how to join the wires together by splicing them, "then

77

slide this rubber tube across the joint so it stays dry. Don't forget to push the rubber tube onto the wire before splicing or else it won't be waterproof."

"If it's that easy why don't ye do it?" asked Johnny.

"Because I must test it by sitting here listening, waiting for you to connect," said the lance corporal. "Time is of the essence. If Jerry attacks, I will not be able to get artillery to respond. Or perhaps I could write a message and run all the way back to echelon, which would save my own arse and…"

"Shut up and tell my sappers where to find t' break in t' line," snapped Johnny.

"I don't know where the break is. They must follow the wires from the rear of the dugout until they come across the break, which could be fifty yards away or one hundred and fifty yards away. They'll know when they reach a crater along their path and look for the broken wires."

"What if your wire is broken five hundred yards away what then?" asked Johnny.

"They keep going until they find it. If they reach the BCR, which means the Buried Cable Route where the line goes underground into multiple junctions, they must turn back because HQ will have already sent cable teams of line men to fix a much more complicated job than our telephone line."

"How would ye know about that?" enquired Johnny.

"Well, if the BCR is smashed, a runner will appear to inform us, but we can't surmise a runner appearing any minute now, we've got to respond immediately because the air line is our responsibility to repair, not the BCR."

"Why call it t' air line?" asked Johnny.

Captain Davidson could not contain himself.

"Will you bloody well get your men along that line instead of discussing the bloody thing?"

Johnny constantly thought about the safety of his men. With bated breath, Johnny blurted out to Captain Davidson.

"Get thy soldiers t' man t' firing steps an' shoot t' shit out o' yon Jerry front line t' keep snipers off my sappers, an' no fuckin' very lights to be fired. We move when thee starts shootin' in five minutes."

"You cannot go with your men, Sergeant Gordon. I forbid it," ordered Captain Davidson. "Even though we have just gained these trenches, that is still no man's land and is overlooked by Jerry snipers. No, you stay here!"

"I will see them off on t' task an' start shootin' when t' infantry opens up on t' enemy," growled Johnny.

"Very well, Sergeant Gordon, move now please," ordered Daffy, as he hurried out of the signals dugout.

The lance corporal led Johnny and his men to where the wires exited the dugout. Keeping low, because standing would mean certain death, he lifted two wires out of the mud and handed one each to Andy and Kinney.

"Hands and knees all the way," said the lance corporal, "and where you see a rise in the ground, leopard crawl. If a star-shell goes up lie still."

The two sappers each carried a coil of wire and a cutting and trimming tool similar to a pair of pliers. They lay on their bellies waiting for the infantry to start shooting. Sporadic firing broke out and they started leopard crawling across no man's land. The lance corporal sneaked back into his dugout as Johnny lay there watching his men crawl across broken ground, fearful of them becoming sitting ducks for Jerry snipers.

Johnny entered the signals dugout to find the lance corporal furiously winding the handle on the field telephone. He listened to the handset and looked up at Johnny.

"Dead as a dodo, Sarge," he said. "I must keep doing this until I connect, or a runner from HQ arrives. I hope never to see a runner from HQ."

"Why?" Johnny asked.

"Because that means the buried cables have been hit and the job of finding and repairing them always costs lives. Jerry is always looking out for linesmen hurrying to fix cables. Communications are crucial on the battlefield."

"Thee talks like an officer wi' yer posh lingo. Ye sounds just like Hellfire Jack. Why ain't thee an officer?" asked Johnny.

The lance corporal stopped winding the handle and set the phone down.

"My father was a colonel and I was earmarked to join his regiment but my older brothers went before me and they were killed. So I decided against my father's wishes and joined the sappers and became a signaller, very dangerous but not as dangerous as being an infantry officer. My father disowned me."

"Thy choice was best fer thee; I've watched umpteen young officers die and thee is still alive, so bollocks t' colonel."

A star shell lit up the night sky and slowly descended illuminating the battlefield. Andy and Kinney lay still, just like the dead soldiers scattered about waiting to be collected after the next advance.

"It'll be feckin' daylight soon," said Andy, "an' they feckin' snipers'll be busy searchin' fer movin' wounded so pray fer no more feckin' star shells."

Kinney's eyes glittered in the light of the star shell but without moving his head toward Andy he talked into the mud.

"There's somethin' movin' ta oor front an' I cannae make it oot."

Both men looked intently to their front and suddenly an arm raised up and waved. A coughing, gurgling sound accompanied the waving arm. Then a wounded soldier sat upright waving at them gurgling louder and louder. Over their heads and between them they heard the snap of the sniper's bullet pass them and crash into the face of the wounded soldier knocking him flat back into the mud. The star shell snuffed out and the two sappers immediately crawled forward into the sudden darkness searching for the break in the line. Crawling over broken ground carrying a coil of wire cable over one shoulder while the other hand felt along the inactive telephone line took a heavy toll on elbows and knees, particularly when doing it for over an hour in the middle of a battlefield. At last they arrived at what looked like a shell crater partially full of water. Rather than getting wet they pulled on their respective cables and out of the water came the broken ends.

"Ye hold ma cable while I crawl around the rim and find t' other cable ends," said Andy, "Fuck knows how this water got in there, it ain't feckin' raining."

He set off around the crater leaving Kinney holding the two cables. Looking at Kinney from the opposite side of the crater Andy stage whispered.

"I'll need to go look for them, they ain't feckin' 'ere."

Andy scrambled about searching and disappeared along the path where the cable should have been. After a few minutes scrambling he found the broken telephone wires. He pulled out the cutting tool, cut and pared the wires and pushed on the little rubber tube before connecting his wire to the brown coloured wire. Finally he covered the joint with the little rubber tube thereby waterproofing it. He played his cable out and made his way back to Kinney.

"Gi' me yon brown cable and connect thy cable t' black 'n, an' I'll go back wi' thine ta connect wi' black 'n on t' other side," said Andy.

The two sappers trimmed and connected the relevant cables to each other and left the remaining cable at the edge of the crater then started crawling back.

"Yippee! We're connected," cried the lance corporal as he held the handset to his ear.

Johnny heard the triumphant shout and joined him in the dugout.

"We're working again," laughed the lance corporal, "bloody great!"

Johnny leaned over him and spoiled the moment.

"Get fuckin' drop shorts t' shit on t' Hun right now. I want my men back all in one piece. I need t' see yon fuckin' trench disintegrate in t' next twenty minutes, fuckin' nonstop."

The lance corporal wound the handle and made the connection and got through to the artillery battery commander who responded with salvo after salvo of shrapnel.

"That'll keep their bloody heads down," shouted the lance corporal at the grinning Johnny.

81

Andy and Kinney could move along the ground much faster without carrying coils of wire and holding up the inactive telephone wire, so made it back safely to the front line and their proud sergeant.

"Send t' grenade team soon, sir, I need t' check their grenades afore goin' through t' tunnel," was Johnny's parting shot to Captain Davidson.

The darkest hour, dusk, the light before dawn was creeping across no man's land. Ten infantrymen scrambled into the crater at the tunnel entrance. They carried sacks of grenades and rifles. The corporal in charge looked bewildered.

"Where are t' rest of t' men?" he asked Johnny.

"Yer fuckin' standin' on 'em," Johnny replied.

The corporal looked down to see a dead hand by his boot. Johnny took charge now and the infantrymen gathered round.

"Right, ye lot. Give each of my men two of thy grenades. When we break through, you lot go to t' right and we go t' left. Get the machine guns first. Yer mates'll be kilt if ye don't. Savvy?"

The infantrymen pulled out grenades from their sacks and handed them around to the sappers, who immediately checked pins and fuses. Their alacrity with anything explosive always impressed young soldiers as grenades were stripped and checked. Johnny checked his watch and started counting down from ten. An ear-jangling silence, then Johnny hit the plunger and blew the charge. A terrific blast of noise and debris came flying out of the tunnel. Like rats up a spout the men disappeared into the dreadful, smoking tunnel. In the black hole they were bent double as they charged through.

The journey through the tunnel was hell for the infantrymen, but the sappers were used to this and knowing what to expect they carried spades and picks to deal with the debris at the German end. Cordite fumes hung thick in the air and the infantrymen coughed their guts up. The sappers geed them up as they stumbled on to where the explosion had blown a massive crater. The light of dawn provided a feeling of relief and fear as the sappers tore into the remaining blockage with picks and spades until the hole was big enough for egress. Johnny was first through the hole and quickly scanned up and down the trench. The new light of dawn provided a beautiful clear sky as he gulped the fresher air of the French countryside. Mutilated soldiers were littered all around. Two stunned snipers with telescoped rifles tried to bring their weapons to bear on Johnny, who showed no mercy and shot them both in the head. This part of Trones Wood was now treeless but the German machine guns were still firing into the advancing British infantrymen from heavily fortified bunkers. The infantrymen cursed and screamed and died as they tripped over the wire entanglements in no man's land. Johnny screamed at the soldiers.

"Fuckin' move! Move! Move! Get yer fuckin' grenades into the fuckin' machine guns. Move! Move!"

They scurried out of the tunnel like a plague of rats - the sappers went left as the grunts went right. There was absolute chaos as they found their bearings and sought out their targets. The early morning sun of the French high summer shone on the carnage below. British soldiers entangled on the barbed wire of the battlefield died in droves as the Germans in Trones Wood swept the crater-riven ground with machine gun fire.

The first line of trenches on the outskirts of the wood was now exposed because of the artillery barrage that had begun again with a creeping barrage that started at the treeline. The sappers and grenade team had cleared the first German trench. What was left of the first wave of infantrymen fell breathlessly into the trench where the officer, Daffy, having survived the awful charge across no man's land, crouched amongst dead men with his teeth chattering on a warm summer morning frightened out of his wits. He tried to stand as Johnny put his hands on his shoulder and tried to calm him.

"Stay down, sir. Take deep breaths, in through yer nose an' out through yer mouth. Deep. Deep. We'll move soon enough."

The noise of the creeping barrage eased slightly as its curtain of fire moved further into the wood. The men were on the fire step awaiting the order to advance. They all knew the score. Follow the creeping barrage to the next line of trenches. Johnny removed his hand.

"Time to go, sir."

Daffy pulled out his whistle and Johnny yanked it from him.

"Tha doesn't need that fuckin' thing. Just fuckin' go. I'm right with thee and so are yer men."

Over the top they went and scores of infantrymen followed. The creeping barrage was supposed to have destroyed the German barbed wire but most of it was still intact and the men became entangled looking like they were treading grapes as they died. As Johnny charged he could see explosions splintering trees and Germans flying high into the air but machine guns were still firing from heavily fortified dugouts. Men fell dead all around him and his lungs were bursting for breath as he ran like hell. A dead soldier entangled across barbed wire provided him with a stepping-stone to cross it then he fell head first into a shell crater.

"Fuckin' 'ell!"

Johnny scrambled to the rim where Daffy appeared alongside him, eyes like ping-pong balls. The trench was twenty yards away. He pulled the pins on two grenades. Daffy's eyes grew wider. First grenade in the air – second now airborne – other men copied – it was raining grenades – coal scuttle helmets – Webley pistol firing at them – into the trench shooting with one hand stabbing with the other. The hand-held bayonet sliced into the windpipe of the screaming German and the light of life died in his terrified eyes as the steel was yanked out and Johnny took stock of what was going on around him.

Hand to hand fighting increased blood lust in the superior force of the attackers as they shot, slashed and hacked their way along the trench. Grey-clad Germans lay all around, their human flesh turned to bloody pulp by the artillery shells, which were still crashing down further into the trees. No neat little holes in tunics here, just blood, guts, heads, limbs and the heart-wrenching screams of wounded soldiers.

Johnny stepped up to the fire step. Enemy fire was now sporadic but he took no chances as he tapped a helmet with his bayonet and the soldier handed it to him. Johnny raised the helmet on his bayonet up over the parapet and cautiously peeped out across into the remaining trees. Trones Wood was being pulverised by the creeping barrage but a machine gun was still firing from a heavily fortified dugout to Johnny's front and further along another bunker hid more machine gunners.

"Our long range snipers do well with their bloody great shells, but not well enough," muttered Sergeant Johnny Gordon.

His men, the sappers, were all in the trench, busy filling rifle magazines. Despite the chaos there was a feeling of huge energy and vigour. Further along the trench the infantrymen were in a state of shock and despair after their baptism of fire, having suffered terrible losses in their valiant effort to get where they were now. These were mainly inexperienced youngsters from various Lancashire towns who were quick to copy the sappers preparing for the next charge across no man's land into the petrified wood.

Johnny found Daffy, the officer, white faced and leaning against the trench wall. Johnny had seen this many a time since coming to France and he knew what to do.

"Good show, sir. Ye led thy men wi' panache. Now we must hold t' line here, as ye well knows, so…"

"What do you want, Sergeant?"

His cursory tone was nothing to Johnny. He barely looked up from his open ciggy packet as he put one in his mouth and lit it. Their eyes met through the smoke. Daffy broke the stare as a shell exploded nearby. But the tension between them was palpable. Johnny offered a ciggy but Daffy declined. Johnny's hard eyes narrowed as they sought out Daffy's through the smoke. He spoke with authority and experience to the officer.

"These trenches have been 'ere for months, so there must be communication trenches between 'ere an' the enemy in t' woods. Me an' my men will go left, an' I'm askin' you to send some of your men

85

t' right so we're not taken by a surprise counter attack, which the Bosch always do."

Daffy braced up, straightened his tunic, checked his Webley pistol and looked along the trench to where his men were busy charging magazines. Johnny noticed some of the infantrymen had the thousand-yard stare, the precursor to shellshock. They were not talking to each other because they did not know what to say. They were charged with adrenaline and fear. Dumbstruck novices to the battlefield, mere teenagers, the flower of English youth far from their Lancashire homes, wondering how the fuck they got themselves into this uncommon predicament that beggared belief and description.

Daffy looked back into the hard eyes of Johnny and knowing he was being judged he smothered the flicker of uncertainty.

"Keep 'em busy, sir, takes their minds off what they've just done," Johnny smiled knowingly.

"Very good, Sergeant. Report back to me in twenty minutes please."

Corporal Taff saw Johnny about turn and knowing what was next, shouted.

"Right, boyo's, move out and remember, do not pick up any souvenirs, and don't bunch up."

The sappers grabbed their kit and tactically moved along the trench. Corporal Taff led the way as Johnny kept up the rear. Dead men in grey tunics littered the trench and were trodden on, first by Taff and then by the others. Johnny glanced back at Daffy's men his hard eyes softened momentarily then back to flintiness just in time to shoot a 'dead' body as it fumbled with a grenade. Grabbing the grenade he threw it over the top into no man's land. Crump! He hardly heard it over the din of exploding shells in Trones Wood. He shot the grey-clad body in the head as he passed and then shot another German who he thought was feigning death.

"Take nowt for granted," he grumbled.

Following his men along the zigzag trench Johnny smirked at the aids to comfort cut into the walls of the long-standing trench - long shelves for sleeping on, places for books and even photos of family groups. Even the smell of ersatz[17] coffee still mingled with the cordite.

The men to the front halted and Johnny clambered past them to reach Taff who held his arm out stiffly to prevent further advance. He was at a junction in the trench, which they recognised immediately as a communication trench running at right angles to the trench they were in and leading into Trones Wood. Taff held out a helmet on a bayonet. A sniper's bullet ricocheted off it. Johnny handed him a German helmet and mimed to do it again, slowly. The helmet slowly went into the view of the sniper and was slowly withdrawn unharmed. Johnny whispered.

"That confused the bastard. Now put t' other back out."

Taff dropped the German helmet and held out his own again. Nothing. Taff slowly withdrew the helmet.

"Yere's a crafty boyo or he's legged it into the woods," said Taff.

Johnny looked quickly about and amongst the dead was a slim young German. The men's eyes followed his and immediately Andy and Kinney scrambled over and lifted it up - they had done this before. Taff put his helmet on the dead German and they leaned him out into view. The head was torn apart by the fusillade of bullets crashing through the trench. They let the body fall into full view and the shooting ceased as the field grey uniform was exposed to the enemy. Johnny poked Solly and Brummie.

"Get back to the sigs bloke an' tell 'im to bring back the drop shorts to the western edge of phase two, drop a marker first. When thou's done that see what Daffy is up to."

The two sappers scampered off back along the trench and the others relaxed as Johnny sat on a firing step and lit up a ciggie.

"Sithee, Sarge, can we open our letters from 'ome now? I haven't had chance to read mine yet and wi' what's happening around 'ere, I may never get to read it," Allballs piped up.

---

[17] ersatz - substitute; synthetic; artificial

Johnny sighed wearily.

"It's rainin' fuckin' artillery shells an' thee wants to read?"

Johnny pulled an unopened letter from his tunic pocket and looked at it.

"Yeah, fuckin' good idea; think about 'ome in all this shit."

They all laughed at the ridiculousness of it all and the gallows humour continued as Kinney pulled out French francs from his letter.

"Aw, Kinney, last time you had frog money you went sick wi' a drippy dick an' moaned when ye had to piss," Andy could not resist the banter.

"She said she needed the money for her wee yins," cried Kinney. "How was I t' ken she was on t' game?"

"She speaks English then, boyo?" asked Taff.

"She did'na say oot," said Andy, "she was dead. She must have been to take him on. Look at him. Feckin' ugly dis'na do him justice."

Johnny looked at his men with hidden pride. They never failed to impress him. Each of them read their letters from home as he read their faces and each in turn brought him joy. Warriors.

He carefully opened his letter and pulled out a single sheet a glimpse of the spidery writing, *Darling Johnny.* His face drained of colour. His men looked at each other concerned. He read it again. His men looked on expectantly.

"Bad news, boyo?" asked Taff.

Johnny raised his gaze and saw his men looking back at him. He seemed to be somewhere else, not here in this maelstrom of exploding shells and mutilated bodies. Then he quickly came back to reality.

"It's, er, from my wife, er... I have a son... Johnny. Born some weeks ago. Apparently he wasn't very well but he's well enough now for her to tell me about him," he stuttered.

The men reacted instantly with backslapping and congratulations but there was still a shadow of consternation on his face. They all felt a bit uncomfortable.

"How's yer wife, boyo, she okay?" asked Taff.

He seemed to snap out of it now and smiled at them.

"Yeah, she's fine, Taff. I didn't know she was pregnant. She kept it from me because of antics 'ere in France. Didn't want me to worry. Wants me to come 'ome all in one piece."

They all smiled, as Solly and Brummie returned along the trench running hard and out of breath.

"The marker... gotta see the marker... should be here any second... here it comes," Solly put his weapon down and gasped for breath.

A high-pitched whining heralded the arrival of the incoming artillery shell. A terrific explosion along the connecting trench excited the men.

"Gotta be a direct hit," said Johnny, as Brummie ran like hell back along the trench to inform the sigs man about the direct hit and to send a salvo.

"It'll rain shells in a minute just over there. That right, Sarge?" asked Solly.

An expression of doubt crossed Johnny's face and he shouted.

"Move back along t' trench in case there's a fuckin' drop short. C'mon! Move! Fuckin' run!"

They quickened their pace as they heard the incoming whine and then the deafening roar of exploding shells amongst the enemy just across the way. A single shell landed right where they were standing, completely destroying the junction of the trenches and bowling them all over as they ran. In a stunning silence the men picked themselves up and shook off the dirt then checked for casualties. Very slowly the noise of battle returned, as did Brummie.

Johnny crossed himself as he got up with blood running down his neck along with grit and soil trapped under his helmet. Brummie rushed past his pals to reach Johnny, who was dusting himself down and about to remove his helmet. Brummie was panting.

"Quick, Sarge, it looks like Jerry has counter-attacked through communication trenches along the line. Daffy sent for you, so..."

"Sent fer fuckin' me? He shoulda sent fer t' fuckin' drop shorts, the twat."

He glared at his men and picked out Solly.

"You go tell t' sigs bloke t' get t' artillery t' drop a cluster at t' eastern end of phase two. No markers, just a cluster. Then tell Daffy we're attacking Jerry in the phase two trench. C'mon, boys, back to work."

Throwing caution to the wind Johnny charged back along to the cratered junction and scrambled across into the enemy communication trench, which was still hung with cordite fumes. With his sappers close on his heels he arrived at the junction with the main trench. It was totally unrecognisable with body parts strewn across the craters, the detritus of artillery shelling. The creeping barrage continued further into the woods, leaving destruction in its wake. Along the trench could be heard shouting and the chattering noise of a firefight. Johnny halted his men and signalled to be quiet. They listened. The creeping barrage stopped. They waited. They waited. Then it happened. The familiar whine of incoming shells filled the air as the requested cluster was delivered right on cue into the grey-clad enemy along the trench. Just a second and the creeping barrage continued again into Trones Wood leaving behind the horrors of trench warfare.

Johnny and his sappers skirmished along the trench dispatching the occasional grey-clad body that moved. A couple of well-placed snipers were busy killing Daffy's men along the communication trench. Johnny lobbed a grenade into the nearest hide and killed two Germans. There was one more hide to go. Johnny's field craft was second to none as he moved over disrupted earth toward the hide. Nearly there, near enough to chuck a grenade. Crawling like a lizard he stopped. A furrow of earth confronted him. To crawl over this ridge would expose him to the enemy in the woods.

"Fuckin' 'ell!"

In a bunker at the edge of the woods a grey-clad machine gunner pointed to where he saw a movement in no man's land. His loader urged him to keep shooting at Daffy's men in the communication trench. The machine gunner kept stopping to look at the ridge of earth hiding Johnny. Just to satisfy himself he fired a burst at the ridge in no man's land just as Johnny was about to slither over it. Johnny had made up his mind and had started to move when he heard a baby cry. Puzzled, he remained still, as the top of the ridge was disintegrated by machine gun fire.

"Fuckin' 'ell!"

Motionless, apart from the expression of disbelief and absurdity crossing his dirty face, he waited for his sappers to deal with the fortified bunker, but everything had changed. Johnny's world had just turned upside down. Suddenly there was a baby in his life plucking at his heartstrings. Rattled to the core his brain went in to overdrive as he tried to come to grips with what had just happened. He began to mutter.

"Did Lord Jesus make that happen? Did he use my new son to warn me? Great Lord of the universe, I thank thee for saving my life. Thou must have a special task for me as many thousands of men have perished on these poppy fields of France. So why me?"

He pulled out his crucifix from around his neck and kissed it. Exploding grenades in the machine gun nest brought Johnny back down to earth and he quickly led his men further along the trench to kill more Germans.

The German machine gun fire that Johnny was about to attack pinned down Captain Davidson's position. The infantrymen only shielded themselves as best they could. Men used dead bodies as cover from the withering fire from their front. The zigzag design of the trench provided some cover but the firepower aimed at Daffy's men took its toll. Daffy tried to think his way out of the situation. Love of England was a strong driving force for the officer class but fear bore down on him in the shape of German machine gun bullets leading to despair. Panic shaped his face and he looked about him like a lost soul. He glanced back along the route of retreat, which was as risky as advancing. All around him his men lay dead. Where were Sergeant Gordon and his sappers? Looking at the Webley pistol shaking in his hand, a crouching soldier opposite jerked his thumb backwards. Daffy shouted but could not be heard over the din of battle, so he screamed.

"Go back! Fuckin' retreat!" the sudden silence seemed to amplify his shouting.

"Go back, go fuckin' back. Fuckin' 'ell, sir, they've fuckin' stopped!"

Daffy's face changed to a suicidal rage and he screamed.

"Charge! Forward men!"

With his whistle in his mouth he blew for all he was worth. Stumbling forward, clambering over the dead, he tripped and fell flat on his face in the blood and muck. The headlong rush of soldiers trampled him in the confined space of the trench floor. A passing boot kicked the back of his head and knocked him unconscious. Minutes later he felt rough hands lifting him. Sergeant Johnny Gordon helped him up and shoved him to the side of the trench where Taff and Brummie supported him.

"Yer all right now, sir. Bloody good show. Yer men have secured the forward trench an' are standin' by waiting for ye." Johnny patted him down looking for wounds, "Some of the men think thee's been shot, sir, but ye looks all in one piece t' me so let's have a ciggie an…"

"You disobeyed a direct order in the field! That means a firing squad for you, Sergeant bloody Gordon," snarled Daffy.

"I am putting you under arrest for cowardice in the face of the enemy," he added.

With a trembling hand he pointed his pistol at Johnny, who dismissed Brummie with a nod. Brummie trotted back to join the sappers on the front line.

"My men just saved thy life, ye stupid man," said Johnny. "We silenced the guns that were killin' ye all."

Daffy looked at Taff.

"Corporal, take his pistol. Escort him to Battalion HQ. He is under arrest. Follow me."

With a sardonic grimace he set off along the trench away from his men. Johnny and Taff walked behind him. They rounded the corner of the zigzag trench and Taff called Daffy to halt.

"Now listen yere, boyo. We just saved your toffee-nosed life and ye thank us by putting our hero sergeant yere in front of a firing squad."

Daffy about turned and aimed his pistol at Taff's face.

"I gave a direct order for you lot to join me in the attack. I should have known better than to rely on your bunch of scruffy clodhoppers," said Daffy.

"Our clodhopping sergeant yere has the DCM for gallantry in the field and you are envious and bitter. Your men are lions led by a donkey. You are callous, vain and..."

"Shut up! You damned Welsh gypsy, or I will escort both of you to..."

The continuing bombardment drowned the noise of Taff's Webley pistol as Daffy's brains flew out of the back of his head taking his hat with it. They immediately checked for witnesses. There were none. Wordlessly they dragged him to a nearby fire step.

"Right-o, boyo, I'll tell the men to beware of the sniper. Good men died because of that toffee-nosed bastard and we..."

"Forget it. C'mon, back to the men an' I never want t' hear DCM mentioned ever again. Got it?"

"Right-o, boyo, never again."

Off they went back to their sappers and a tale of woe for the infantrymen.

CHAPTER SIX

The advance had halted on this part of the front line to allow fresh troops to reinforce the front line and the logistics to catch up with bedraggled and hungry soldiers. Apart from the artillery barrage, which had somewhat slackened, the only other noise was the sporadic firing from further afield in either direction along the front line. The sappers were hunkered down making a brew and a meal during the lull in fighting.

An infantry corporal warily approached Johnny as he swigged his tea.

"Sithee, Sergeant, I am the senior soldier right now because my officer and all of the sergeants are dead or dying out there somewhere wounded."

Johnny put down his mug of tea and stood to face the corporal. He felt weary and strained but cheered up for the corporal. He put his hand on his shoulder and their helmets clinked as their heads touched.

"Right, lad, thee's in charge until we get relieved in t' mornin'. Savvy?"

"I didn't know that, Sarge," the corporal replied.

Johnny pulled a sketched map from his tunic and showed it with his finger poking at a line. The corporal looked on puzzled.

"See that line?" said Johnny. "It's just over there in t' woods and when we're sittin' there in t' mornin' suppin' a brew we get relieved."

"But Sarge, that's a hundred yards away an' there's bunkers an' dugouts all over t' show out there."

"Aye, lad, an' tomorrow we'll be in 'em suppin' t' brew."

The corporal jumped with fright as a massive explosion threw earth and body parts high into the blue sky. The tunnel mine was so powerful, it sucked the breath out of the sappers and nearby infantrymen. Torsos, heads, legs and arms rained down fifty yards away to the right of Johnny's position. Johnny grabbed the corporal's shoulder.

"Are your men over there?" he asked.

"Those poor bastards are the Manchester Pals Battalion. They're in line abreast of us but we haven't enough men to link up with them. There's a bit of a gap between us," he replied.

"The gap looks to be a bit bigger now so spread your men out further an' prepare for a counter attack," ordered Johnny.

The corporal departed as grim faces gathered around Johnny. Taff pushed through with two steaming mugs of tea.

"This is the last brew. We need to send somebody back for more tea," he said.

"That can wait," said Johnny, "we need to recce along the trench. These tunnel mines 'ave been 'ere fer weeks if not months so there'll be tell-tale signs directly opposite, so take Solly, Tat an' Allballs. Yers know what to look for."

Without a word Taff, Allballs, Tat and Solly headed off to the west. Johnny gestured Kinney and Andy to move east, toward the Manchester Pals positions.

"Fifty yards max an' don't get caught up wi' t' Manchesters. Come straight back to me once you've checked that fuckin' crater."

They disappeared along the trench as Johnny beckoned Brummie and Yiggs

"Get me Fritz's tin hat."

They did not have far to go for one of those. Yiggs yanked the helmet off a dead German as Brummie brandished his bayonet and Yiggs tossed it accurately onto the bayonet then Brummie handed it to Johnny who slowly poked it over the parapet. Nothing. He took off his helmet and whistled along the trench so that nearby soldiers could see it was him about to don a German helmet. He spoke to his men.

"I need to see what lies twixt 'ere an' t' next trench. Fuckin' wire was still intact on t' last charge. Cost a lot o' men."

Johnny sneaked a peak across no man's land and saw broken trees, disrupted earth, shell craters, splintered bunkers in the ravaged wood, exploding shells beyond the next trench line and just twenty yards in front a rat disappearing down a wooden hatch - a dugout.

"Fuckin' 'ell!"

The constant din of shelling ceased momentarily and he heard a baby cry. Dropping like a stone to his knees he ripped off the helmet and stared at his shaking hands in the muck next to Brummie.

"Fuckin' 'ell, Sarge. You look ill. What did you see? I could 'ave swore I heard a baby cry. Did you...?" Brummie remarked.

In a trice Johnny grabbed hold of Brummie's tunic. Their noses touched as Johnny shouted into his face.

"Say that again about a baby cry?"

Utterly taken aback by Johnny's behaviour he shouted back.

"I heard a fuckin' baby cry. I thought I heard it before but didn't say ought cos ye might think I'm fuckin' shell shocked."

Johnny backed off and straightened Brummie's webbing straps and bullet pouches. His face remained puce but normal colour was quick to return.

"Ye heard it before? Did t' others hear it? Are ye pulling my leg?" Johnny asked.

"No, Sarge, I'm not pulling thy leg. Nobody mentioned it but I wondered if it was a Bosch trick to entice us into no man's land."

"Bollocks, they ain't that sick," said Johnny, "but there's gotta be an explanation."

Kinney and Andy returned exhausted from their recce.

"Yon Manchester boys are in ribbons, Sarge," said Andy, "I don't know what to think, so many of them killed."

"Aye," said Kinney, "Fritz is showin' 'is true colours the noo wi' 'is dirty tricks."

"What dirty tricks?" snapped Johnny.

The artillery barrage intensified but much nearer to their position and the earth trembled beneath their feet as Johnny shouted.

"They're givin' t' area another goin' over, must be a lot o' wire out there. What dirty tricks, Kinney?"

Kinney shouted back.

"Sergeant Major o'er yonder says a baby was found an' they all gathered round to see it. Fritz knew they would, dirty bastards."

The sappers' revulsion was etched in their faces as the barrage continued around them. Falling debris made them crouch low in the trench.

Taff, Allballs, Tat and Solly scurried around the zigzag corner to join them. Their grim faces heralded bad news.

"We're to hold this position while fresh troops arrive for the next advance, which is a night attack at zero two hundred hours tonight," said Taff.

"Who said?" asked Johnny.

"Beyond the Liverpool Regiment to the west, or what's left of them, are my countrymen the 39th Welsh Division," said Taff. "Fuckin' hard boyos they be too. A Cap'n told me to pass it along until field telephones catch up with us. But for sure it's tonight boyo."

Johnny frowned enigmatically. Taff looked on puzzled.

"What the fuck's the matter now? We've done this a thousand times," he said.

Johnny turned on Kinney and Andy and growled angrily.

"You two, go tell t' Manchesters the good news an' scrounge some tea. See what's left o' that tunnel mine an' if we can use it tonight" He looked at Taff and said, 'There's a dugout twenty yards to our front an' I don't know why it's there. Fuckin' strange things goin' on round 'ere."

The men sat on sleeping shelters cut out of the clay by the Germans. The seemingly never-ending thunder of artillery shells screaming overhead into the wire of no man's land did not faze these men as they fished out their ciggies. Solly pulled out his baccy tin - him being one of the legendary few who could fill a ciggy paper with baccy, roll it, lick it, seal it and light it all with a single flick of his hand. In the maelstrom of trembling earth their grimy faces revealed weariness, indicating a foregone conclusion that death was inevitable and certainly imminent. One lit match was passed from hand to hand to light up as they sat wearily waiting to hear about strange things going on.

"All right then boyo, I can't wait to yere what strange things can happen in a place like this, especially on a lovely sunny day amongst the poppies along the tranquil River Somme."

Taff's banter created little reaction on the surrounding faces as they all looked up at their sergeant then Johnny looked at Brummie.

"We thought we heard a baby cry out there in no man's land," he said.

They all turned to look at Brummie.

"Aye, an' then Kinney an' Andy comes back an' says the Manchester lads got suckered onto a tunnel mine by a cryin' baby. They gathered round to see it an' Fritz blew 'em all up. Fuckin' sick bastards."

"I don't get this fuckin' dugout to our front. It's just a man-sized square hole wi' a wooden frame around it. I can't see its purpose," Johnny said, looking Taff in the eye.

Taff got up to climb the fire step. Johnny stopped him.

"Wait 'til it gets dark, then we'll both see what it is. It might be a tunnel hatch or maybe a bunker ventilation grill."

"Hey, Sarge, we might be sittin' on a fuckin' tunnel mine. What d'ye think, Sarge?" Brummie piped up.

"They would've blown it by now lad, while they had the chance, unless they be waiting on our reinforcements to arrive."

"We 'eard a fuckin' baby cry, Sarge, an' they Manchester lads 'eard one too an' look what happened to them, blown to fuck," said Brummie.

Allballs pulled out what looked like a hunter's horn and lay on the trench floor with it to his ear. Johnny chuckled.

"If thee can hear anything other than our creeping barrage down there, I'll get ye a fuckin' stethoscope fer Christmas and..."

"Sarge, get him a fuckin' enema kit," cried Solly. "He stinks like a fuckin' pole cat cos he's so full o' shit."

"Last time he did that he heard voices, remember?" said Brummie

98

"Aye, it was fuckin' Satan," said Solly, and then in falsetto he sang, "I'm waiting for you, oo, oo."

The gallows humour was lost in the intensified barrage. Johnny had to shout to be heard.

"Brummie, you an' Allballs go back to rear echelon for rations and get me a geophone from our quartermaster. Tell 'im we need more ammonal an' a replacement for Billy Nolan. Scrounge what ye can."

Along the trench where the Manchester lads were killed, Kinney and Andy picked away at the trench wall looking for the tunnel. Kinney slammed his spade into loose earth and fell through after it. They had found the dreaded tunnel. The nearby infantrymen joined in to enlarge the access. They stepped back in amazement and admiration as the two sappers scrambled down into the maw of the earth. Andy shouted at them.

"Stay well back and dinnae block th' hole, we need to breathe doon here."

The sappers disappeared into the gloomy cavern and stood motionless, straining their ears, holding their breath and listening. Knowing the enemy end of the tunnel was blocked did not prevent them from performing their drill. Discipline was paramount in enemy tunnels. They switched on their torches to illuminate the debris stretching out ahead of them. Then came the difficult part of the drill. In numbing silence, the sappers crept forward side by side. Andy's torch shone on the floor while Kinney's shone at head height. The torchlights cut through the hanging cordite fumes as they went. Cautiously, they crept along at a snail's pace looking for booby traps. Andy's torch flashed along a taught wire stretched across the tunnel at ankle height. Both men stepped back in unison and knelt down. Then, on all fours they crawled forward with their hands carefully feeling the floor in front of them. Andy stopped and whispered.

"Good job we didnae go straight for the wire, there's a pressure switch 'ere, just in front o' it."

Kinney grunted.

"Aye, if yon bloody Manchester lads had got in 'ere afore us they'd aw be dead the noo."

"Aye, but just a wee minute while I stick a pin in this bastard an' clear it.'

With his torch in his mouth Andy fiddled with a safety pin to neutralise the pressure switch. Pin inserted. Job done. He carefully lifted the metal device out of the muck as Kinney leant over and plucked the detonator out of the main charge, which was covered in ball bearings and nuts and bolts - antipersonnel.

"Dirty bastards. Now for the trip wire. Its taut so it's a push-pull switch an' it can be on my side or thine, so I'll check my side first. Ye go back if you like?" Kinney whispered.

"Up yer feckin' kilt, just get on wi' it," snarled Andy.

In the torchlight both men's eyes were wide with trepidation as Kinney gingerly felt along the trip wire using finger and thumb whilst holding his weight with his other hand. He held his breath as his right hand slowly snaked into a small cavity in the tunnel wall where his end of the booby trap was hidden from view. Sweat poured down his face and his heart beat in his ears as he carefully withdrew his hand and whispered.

"Ah dinnae ken where the feckin' wire is goin', ah cannae reach the fecker.'

Kneeling he wiped the sweat from his eyes as Andy repeated the process on his side. It was excruciatingly slow and difficult to manipulate his arm around a bend without compromising the trip wire. The seconds ticked away as the sweat dripped off his nose onto his tunic. Andy grunted and cursed.

"Got the wee bastard. It's a push-pull wi' a charge this side an' ye can bet on t' other side too. I'll put a pin in my side an' if ye cannae reach t' other side, we can assume it's a charge wi' oot a switch."

Kinney handed him a safety pin and whispered.

"Ye can assume what the feck ye like but ye ain't cuttin' yon feckin' wire while I'm 'ere, feck ye."

Both men stood up and dusted themselves down.

100

"Awreet, we'll pull it on t' way oot. Put a tinsel on it so we don't feckin' trip o'er it on t' way back," Andy whispered.

Kinney fished out a strip of silver paper and hung it on the wire. They stepped over it and moved on, shining their torches ahead of them. They could only see the fog of fumes hanging hauntingly over the clay floor but on they silently crept, seeking out trip wire and booby traps in the detritus of underground mining, as planks of wood and pit props could hide devices that kill.

At last they arrived at the blocked exit shaft and listened. The muffled sound of German voices could be heard on the other side of the caved in shaft, and a machine gun firing on their left side and then another on their right. They had heard enough so they about turned and crept back to where they left the tinsel on the trip wire. Andy pulled out a wire hook and attached it to a bobbin of twine that Kinney was about to unwind as he crept back to the exit where the Manchester lads awaited them.

Kinney arrived at the exit hole and gave a low whistle. Andy attached the hook to the trip wire and headed back to Kinney. Both men scrambled up the rubble to fresh air, careful not to tighten the twine. Out of harm's way Andy yanked the twine. KABOOM! A hell of a bang and a great chorus of cheers welled up from the German trenches. The sappers' dirty faces cracked with glee as the infantrymen looked on in astonishment.

One young chap stumbled over the rubble.

"Ee bah gum, what were all that about? Them there Jerrys all laughin' an' cheerin' like?" he asked.

"They think they booby-trapped us," Kinney chuckled.

The sappers looked at each other and rolled over laughing. Andy looked at the young chap.

"How long 'as thee been in t' army, lad? Ye dinnae look old enough."

The young chap blushed and stammered.

"Sithee, I joined up wi' my younger brother in May so we've been in t' army for nearly two months now, so…"

The sappers looked at each other in mock amazement.

"His younger feckin' brear!" Andy roared, as they leant on each other laughing their heads off.

The stern faces of the surrounding infantrymen spoiled the fun.

"What?' shouted Kinney.

Another young chap, not wearing a helmet because of a head wound and the blood still seeping from the dirty bandage, spoke.

"Captain Davidson ordered him o'er t' top into machine-gun fire," he looked across at his young companion, "his brother got cut in two."

The two hardened warriors got to their feet with sadness in their eyes and gave the surviving brother a hug. They turned to leave as Andy said to nobody in particular while pointing down the hole.

"Keep yer 'eads down and dinnae allow any fecker doon there. If Fritz starts shelling, yers can shelter in there but dinnae go too far in. Stay doon this end."

Grim faced Andy and Kinney headed back along the trench to join Johnny and the others. Under cover of darkness fresh troops had moved into positions all along the front line. Men and their kit had made lateral movement difficult and annoying to many, especially Sergeant Johnny Gordon. His troop of sappers were resting on their cut-out shelves while Johnny and Taff tested the geophone on the floor of the trench, which also tested their tempers as men passed to and fro constantly.

A tall slender figure loomed up out of the darkness and tripped headlong over the kneeling Taff and fell on top of Johnny. Using his impressive power, Johnny flipped the intruder over his head and adopted a fighting stance, ready to start punching. The slim figure clambered up to stand a good five inches taller than Johnny. This was Second Lieutenant David Anderson the replacement platoon commander, full of enthusiastic inexperience and known by the men as Mr Ando.

"You fuckin' blind twat! What the fuckin' 'ell d' ye think…?"

"Shut up! You bloody clodhopper," snapped Mr Ando, "you are referring to an officer of the line as being a blind something or other. I am Lieutenant Anderson to you and your men, and I am the replacement platoon commander for Captain Davidson. I give the orders here."

He pointed his swagger stick at Johnny and snarled.

"That man there. Step forward and be recognised."

Taff got to his feet as Johnny strode forward and presented his grimy, wild-eyed face within inches of the young officer.

"Royal Engineers section commander, Sergeant Gordon. On detachment to the King's Liverpool Regiment, sir."

Taff's dirty face appeared next to Johnny's with his livid, freshly stitched head wound visible in the poor light of the trench. The young officer's eyes were drawn to it.

"Now listen yere, boyo. You not lookin' where you're goin' knocked my wounded head, thereby risking our forward patrol when it gets darker and…"

"Stand to attention when you speak to me, you filthy object," snapped Mr Ando, now looking at Johnny, "I know nothing about patrols going out tonight. Who ordered it?"

"I did," said Johnny. "I'm going to recce the ground ahead of our position here and the German bunker just here to our front."

"I know nothing about German bunkers near our position. Where is it?"

Johnny pointed at the trench wall.

"Twenty yards that away. The enemy lines are eighty yards further on with machine gun positions directly opposite in several dugouts along our front. They survived the artillery barrage and…"

"Another barrage is due to start," he checked his watch, "in a couple of hours from now, so you will not have much time for patrolling. So I forbid it. Stand down Sergeant until I tell you to move," said Mr Ando.

"We don't operate like that on detachment. As Royal Engineers we use our initiative to save lives and kill the Bosch. A tunnel mine killed the Manchester lads along with some of yours just over there today. So we are charging the tunnel with explosives at the Bosch end of the tunnel to coincide with the advance from here. Thereby killing any Bosch around it and advancing through the tunnel with grenades to attack the machine guns that will cut your men down before you get half way across there."

"The artillery will eradicate that threat, so…"

"That's what Captain Davidson said and hundreds died, so leave the engineering to the engineers and lives will be saved and the Bosch will die in their…"

"I will not have my orders countermanded by you or any other bogtrotter, Sergeant. You will go over the top with the King's or face the firing squad."

With that the subaltern about turned and marched off into the darkness to more shouts of indignation from men further down the line. The sappers' faces showed defiance regarding the inevitability of death should they go over the top or face a firing squad, but their eyes swayed Johnny's decisions, as usual.

"Taff, you go back t' rear echelon t' HQ and tell Hellfire Jack our problem." Johnny looked at Kinney, "You go wi' 'im and tell 'im about the tunnel and that you've already cleared it for tonight's attack."

The two men picked up their weapons and disappeared into the darkness, on their way to find Hellfire Jack. Taff and Kinney soon stood to attention in front of the Chief Clerk, a warrant officer, who was accompanied by a major, Royal Engineers. The Chief Clerk reported to the Major just what Taff had reported to him.

"And that's the problem, sir."

"Well, we can't have popinjay subalterns interfering with experienced men like Sergeant Gordon, can we?" said the Major.

"No, we bloody can't," said Hellfire Jack, as he entered through another door.

There he was, Colonel Sir John Norton-Griffiths of the Royal Engineers, the eccentric millionaire and Member of Parliament for the Conservative Government, dressed immaculately in his tailored uniform with flashing eyes and a trimmed moustache, making him truly handsome and dashing.

"Stand at ease, you two. Chief get a case of good French wine and give it to the Corporal. I heard every word you men said, so take the wine and give it to Johnny Gordon. Oh yes, I know all about you men. You, Taff, should be home in Wales nursing your wounded head, but you are here, fighting for King and country, which means a great deal in my book. Bloody infantry!" He turned to face the Major, "Basil, get a crown for Sergeant Gordon. I am promoting him in the field to Staff Sergeant, and while you're at it, get three stripes for Sergeant Taff Dupree here, what! Congratulations, Taff, you are now a Royal Engineers Senior NCO. Now get yourselves back and deal with that tunnel."

With a furrowed brow he went back into his office muttering something about bloody infantry subalterns. The major returned and gave the men a hessian sack full of bottles of French wine.

"When you get back you can expect a visit from the CO of the Liverpool Lads. The Colonel will be talking to him now. Good luck, men," he said.

The sappers marched out of the HQ and headed for the front line as Hellfire Jack stepped out of his dugout office, which had once belonged to the Germans, its furniture and wooden doors still bedecked with German office paraphernalia.

"Chief, get those men back here first thing tomorrow. They can rest for a day and then on to the start of the new gallery under the Hun HQ. They've done with the bloody infantry. I need their skills in the new tunnel."

The Chief Clerk grabbed a field telephone and furiously wound the side handle for a connection. He spoke to someone in the King's Liverpool Regiment.

The Officer Commanding the Liverpool Lads shook the hand of Staff Sergeant Johnny Gordon, whilst holding a bottle of wine in his other hand. Johnny saluted as the Major scurried away and the sappers relaxed and sat on the ledges grinning at each other as they passed around the bottles of wine.

Johnny good-naturedly tilted Taff's helmet exposing the wound.

"That'll get ye a couple o' pints in t' Sergeants Mess, Taff."

The men smiled at the banter. Solly looked at Johnny and said.

105

"Ha, I hope this doesn't change things with ye two goin' up in t' world?"

"I don't think so," said Johnny. "We're all goin' down in t' world tomorrow, into the bowels of the new tunnel."

"Aye," said Andy, "the sooner the feckin' better we gets away from toffee-nosed feckin' dandies wi' pips on their feckin' shoulders."

"Och aye," said Kinney, "but dinnae ye forget how ye danced aboot laughin' when they pulled us oot o' that last yin tae come 'ere? Feckin' awful hole that was. Lots o' men died doon there."

Solly farted loudly.

"Oh, Jesus fuckin' Christ. No wonder they call ye the poison fuckin' dwarf, yer as cheerful as fuckin' mustard gas," he said.

The laughter died as a familiar tall dark figure loomed into view and looked intently into each mans' face as his lip curled into a snarl.

"Get to your feet when an officer is present, you insolent cowards."

The sappers were stung into anger and were on their feet in a trice; their eyes blazed with rage. Johnny's eyes were locked onto the eyes of the young officer.

"That is twice we have met and each time ye have intimated cowardice to me and my sappers who have had many battles wi' the Hun. You have never yet stepped into no man's land, so make sure ye comes to my men when we occupy that Bosch trench o'er yonder and we'll discuss cowards and how not to be one."

Solly started his repartee, which the men always heartily supported.

"Look how tall he is, Staff? He's head and shoulders o'er his men."

"Aye," said Kinney, "an' ye can bet who the Jerry snipers'll be aiming at."

"An' yonder machine gunners'll be pickin' ye out too, Mr Anderson," said Allballs. "Ye'd best crouch low, especially if we don't get their machine gunners wi' our tunnel mine and…"

"Bollocks" said Taff, "we'll get the machine gunners and the snipers afore 'e's half way across no man's land!"

Staff Sergeant Johnny Gordon stopped the banter, knowing it had hit the mark. His eyes betrayed the hidden smirk aching to crack his fathomless face.

"Sergeant Dupree, get the men down t' hole. Place the charges and prepare to fire. The barrage starts soon an' I want ye all out t' hole afore it begins." Turning to Mr Ando, he added, "It is usual for Platoon Commanders to send a grenade team with us to silence the machine guns, sir."

Taken by surprise Mr Ando harrumphed loudly.

"What! My men are needed for the charge across no man's land, Sergeant, and…"

"Staff Sergeant, Mr Anderson," said Johnny, pointing at the new crown stitched above the three chevrons, "an' if ye aren't sendin' a grenade team through t' tunnel wi' me, you will lose many good men and probably yourself. So…"

"Damn it man! Staff Sergeant why should you be so bloody full of yourself? Preposterous. It…"

"Experience and sapper initiative, sir, plus a long time fightin' t' Bosch underground and in t' trenches. You'd do well to listen to my men, they are all decorated soldiers and survivors."

The chinless wonder stiffened and displayed his stiff upper lip as the sappers moved out along the trench heading for the tunnel. With his swagger stick under his left arm Mr Ando snarled.

"An officer of the line, a platoon commander, does not seek advice from a bunch of barnyard yokels. How dare you suggest such nonsense, you bloody…"

A baby cried.

"Shut up! Listen to that!" hissed Johnny.

Looking at each other incredulously as the sound was drowned by sporadic shellfire. Johnny checked his watch.

"Nearly an hour afore the barrage begins. There's nowt twixt us an' t' Bosch trenches, apart from t' mysterious hole in t' ground out there."

107

"So bloody what?" said Mr Ando. "It is twenty yards away and German snipers are waiting for idiots to investigate because they must have heard it too, and they bloody put it there."

Grim faced Johnny checked his Webley pistol and shone his torch along the sleeping shelves looking for a bayonet and picked one up.

"Would thee like to join me, sir?" he asked Mr Ando.

"Losing an NCO is bad enough," he said, "losing an officer is…"

"That'll be a no then. In that case would ye be kind enough to inform t' gunners to cease firing star shells so I can get out there undetected?" asked Johnny.

Mr Ando looked up to see the night sky illuminated like it was daylight caused by the apocalyptic images of exploding star shells hanging beneath their slowly descending parachutes. He scowled at Johnny and quickly departed to instruct the signallers to inform the artillery to cease fire with the star shells.

Johnny climbed the fire step in readiness to slither over the top and crawl across no man's land to the mysterious hole to his front. Waiting. Waiting. Waiting. Darkness fell the instant the star shells stopped being fired. The Germans, alarmed at the sudden darkness, opened fire with machine guns and sniper fire. German artillery shells also started exploding all across the front, giving the Brits a taste of what was to come.

The broken ground and shell holes provided Johnny with some cover but he moved too fast to care about cover and in just a few seconds he was there, peering down into the darkness. Putting his arm down into the hatch he flicked on his torch and saw it was a dugout with another floor hatch. He pocketed the torch. Slithering his feet into the hole he lowered himself down and dangled a few feet above the earth floor. He dropped and rolled. Holding his breath in the dark silence, listening. He breathed easy as the star shells lit up the sky again, shedding a little light down through the hatch. With pistol drawn he crept to the other hatch. In the flashes of light from above he saw a ladder leading down to the floor below. Holding his breath, he listened - a soft cough, like that of a child or a woman from further below. Fuckin' 'ell how deep is this bunker, he thought.

Deftly stepping onto the ladder, he climbed down to the floor and saw a flicker of light from beneath yet another hatch. Fear gripped him as he stepped on a cable. Crouching, he followed the cable, which disappeared into a pile of earth rubble that he knew was a blocked tunnel. Following the cable in the opposite direction he discovered a massive camouflet [18] chamber packed with explosives. Frenetically he pulled out his torch not caring who saw the light and followed the cable to the detonator and quickly disarmed it. Desperately searching for other cables, he did not see the head come up through the hatch. It was a woman. He very nearly shot her when she spoke English with a French lilt.

"English? You are English? Don't shoot, I am French."

Dropping to his knees he levelled the pistol and torch at her face and held up the cable for her to see.

"Any more of this down there?" he snarled.

"Ah, the telephone wire. Yes, they told us not to touch it until they connect the telephones. It is down here in the main corridor."

"Who is down there?" he snapped.

"Only one baby now, they took the others away, I hid him under my bed. Come, I show you."

Johnny followed down the ladder into a large candlelit corridor where he saw doors opening into what could be described as boudoirs. He followed her into the first one and was taken aback by the splendour. A luxurious bed and couch with wardrobes and a carpeted floor. Looking back along the corridor he could see it was blocked at the far end with rubble.

"That is the telephone cable, it goes through there," she said, pointing at a cable running along the corridor floor.

---

[18] camouflet - in military science, is an artificial cavern created by an explosion. If the explosion reaches the surface then it is called a crater

His eyes followed her pointing finger and like a man possessed he clawed through the rubble covering the camouflet entrance to make a small hole, through which he shone his torch and saw the bomb.

"Fuckin' 'ell!"

Making the hole bigger he scrambled through into the chamber. With his torch he followed the cable into the stack of explosives and saw the initiation set right in the middle of the boxes of explosives. There was not enough room in the chamber to pull the stack apart so he tried to prise the ends of boxes apart to make a gap big enough for him to reach the detonator. The sweat ran down his face and into his eyes but with super human effort his fingers reached the detonator and he slid it out of the gun cotton primer thereby disarming the charge. He quickly checked for other initiation sets and could not see any, but he did see a pull switch connected to the cable running under the boxes of explosives.

"Trust Jerry to booby trap the cable, just like we do."

He shone his torch around for a final look and scrambled back out into the corridor to rejoin the woman.

"Did you see the telephone?" she asked.

"It is a bomb designed to blow after the first bomb to kill the rescuers. Dirty Jerry bastards. What're ye doin' 'ere anyway?" he asked.

"This is a brothel for the men in this sector. They were having a wonderful time and then you English arrived. They told us you would never get this far."

It then dawned on her what he had just said and she started screaming.

"A bomb? A bomb! What are we to do? Aghhh!"

Johnny grabbed her and clamped his hand over her mouth. That was the moment her perfume and slenderness aroused him. Something primal, deep in his guts disturbed him.

"Shh. Be quiet now. We don't want Jerry to hear us. I will take thee to safety very soon." He checked his watch, "Where's the baby?"

She grabbed his hand and led him back to the bedroom where she stooped to pull a bundle of clothing from under the bed and opened the bundle to reveal the pretty pink face of the baby. In the magic of the moment he removed his helmet and embraced the woman and baby. She kissed him passionately and he felt weak at the knees. His world was upside down as she placed the baby on the couch and again kissed him and pulled him to the bed. The same primal drive as Johnny's exploded within her and she decided to grab what she could before the end.

"You are a Godsend and I can only reward you by making love. But I feel also that this maybe the last time I ever make love. I sense no future for me but for the baby… he lives."

Without a pause Johnny swiftly shed his tunic as she undressed to reveal great beauty. They both fell on the bed, kissing and passionately embraced as she opened her legs and brought her knees up so Johnny could enter her swiftly and fully. The exquisite motions of the experienced prostitute sent any guilty thoughts of Jinny into outer space. She used her inner muscularity to give Johnny the sexual experience of a lifetime as they made torrid love and their emotions crashed through them like never before. Johnny lay looking at the boarded ceiling knowing it hid clay. Thoughts about the absurdity of it all made him whisper.

"Ye must have something special in store for me, Lord Jesus."

He checked his watch.

"Times up! Get dressed, quickly. We have very little time," he said, "we must get back to our lines."

She was dressed before he was, but he moved and dressed all at the same time.

"Grab the baby, the barrage starts any minute now!" he shouted.

Terror-stricken at Johnny's haste she grabbed the baby from the bed and followed Johnny up the ladder. He reached down and yanked her up through the hatch and off he went up the next ladder followed by the screaming duo. Again he roughly pulled her through the hatch and lay down to reach for the ladder to use to escape through the final hatch into no man's land. Placing the ladder beneath the hatch he raced up it and with his bayonet raised his helmet above the hatch - nothing. The woman and baby were right behind him on the ladder.

"Give me the baby when I get out. Do not stand up, ye must crawl behind me to safety, now move!'

Slithering out onto the broken ground he reached back and grabbed the baby from the woman just as the first shells arrived to pulverise no man's land.

"Fuck this!"

He got up and ran with the baby. The screaming woman tried in vain to catch up and was vaporised by exploding shells. Her instincts were spot on. That was the moment the baby fell silent in Johnny's arms. The continuous unbroken rhythm of the artillery guns heralded Johnny's arrival to his men waiting anxiously for him. Sliding over the parapet he passed the baby like a rugby ball to Solly.

"Catch 'im!" he shouted.

Solly caught the flying bundle of rags as Johnny crashed into the trench wall and dropped to his knees. The men were dumbstruck by the new arrival.

"Fuckin' 'ell, Staff, we 'aven't gorra uniform to fit this little fella," shouted Solly, "Worra we gonna do wi' 'im?"

"His mother's behind me," shouted Johnny. "Where the hell is she?"

"On her way to t' angels, Staff," shouted Andy, "Ye only made it by t' skin of your teeth. What t' hell happened?" he asked.

"Aye, Staff, at least ye saved the wee yin," shouted Kinney. "Solly! Gi' 'im a suck on yer teat, he likes ye, mon. Ah cannae wait ta hear this feckin' story."

Taff arrived with Allballs fairly out of breath.

"Charges are set an' ready to blow, boyo! What the hell's that boyo? Bloody hell man, we can't take that wi' us," Taff shouted.

"An' he can't stay here," Solly shouted back.

"Sithee, Staff," said Allballs, "back yonder is a horse's nose-bag, should I run back and...?"

"Fuckin' run now. Go!" shouted Johnny.

Wild-eyed Allballs raced away along the trench as the others gathered around the baby, completely ignoring the crashing artillery shells exploding just a few yards away. Johnny looked at the faces of his men gazing down at the soft pink face, knowing they would want an explanation. The hard eyes that had witnessed prolonged indescribable carnage soften in the light of bursting star shells and high explosive heavy artillery shells. Johnny was totally bemused as he watched his men fawn over the baby.

"Solly, thee 'n Allballs follow us through t' tunnel," he shouted, then at Taff, "the rest of us move out now. C'mon!"

The sappers raced away along the trench to the east to where the Manchester Lads were killed and where Staff Sergeant Johnny Gordon planned his revenge. Gathered around the tunnel entrance were a dozen infantrymen carrying sacks of grenades. The sappers arrived and Johnny took charge. In the light of the star shells the men shared the grenades, checked fuses and pins and then squirrelled them away into various tunic pockets and bullet pouches. Brummie scrambled down into the tunnel and connected the pared wire ends to the plunger all ready to blow. Young infantrymen looked on, eyes wide with fear, as they obeyed Johnny's instructions to pull down their helmets over their eyes. Johnny checked his watch and chanted.

"Wait for it… wait… wait."

The shelling ceased.

"Brummie!"

Brummie pressed the plunger as Johnny stood and watched the Germans head skywards. The back blast knocked some of the men over and Johnny screamed.

"Go, go, go fuckin' move!"

The men scrambled down into the tunnel and all along the front whistles blew as thousands of men went over the top.

Torches flashed in the nightmare charge through the tunnel. The men raced along doubled over because of the low headroom. The fumes hung heavy and they coughed their hearts out. Some of them screamed in fear of their lives. The sappers' discipline controlled the

113

calamity as they dashed through the tunnel geeing the grunts along in this deepest circus of hell - this would remain in the minds of the survivors forever. The sappers cleared the exit into the German trench where now a new crater existed, with dead men littered all along the rim and beyond. Johnny controlled the flow of wild-eyed men, grunts to the right and sappers to the left. They clawed their way over remnants of mutilated bodies. The soldiers sought out their enemy and with bloody hands they pulled pins and hurled grenades as they advanced along the German trench. Johnny sent his men along the trench to the left.

"No further than fifty yards!" he shouted.

Stooping back down into the tunnel he heard Solly and Allballs approach.

"Solly! Stay in t' mouth o' t' tunnel just out o' t' fumes an' wait fer me," he shouted.

"Right-o," came the reply.

Johnny climbed a firing step to look back across no man's land at the advancing British being mown down by German machine guns and snipers. As he looked along the trench he saw the grenade teams hurl their grenades into fortified dugouts killing machine gunners and grey-clad soldiers. Death was everywhere.

A new creeping barrage began just a few yards in front of the captured German trench. The destruction of Trones Wood continued just as Solly and Allballs reached the trench opening onto the crater. Solly wore the horse's nosebag on his back just like a papoose with the baby fitted snugly inside, not making a sound as Allballs fussed along behind. Johnny dropped down beside him as screaming infantrymen fell and dived into the trench, relieved to be out of no man's land and the withering line of fire.

"Solly, stay in t' tunnel entrance," shouted Johnny. "The first infantrymen are just gettin' 'ere, lots of wounded. We go no further than this bloody tunnel. Jerry'll start shellin' us any minute now. Bastards!"

As though Johnny had prompted it German artillery shells exploded amongst the stragglers in no man's land. With shrapnel whistling by overhead the cries of the wounded were heard between exploding shells. Johnny was heartbroken witnessing the stupendous loss of Lancashire youth in this horrendous battle, as more young men dived, leaped and fell into the trench, wearing expressions of wild fear on their dirty young faces.

Taff and the other sappers squeezed past the growing numbers of infantrymen to arrive back at the tunnel. They blocked the entrance so nobody could enter. The baby was their secret.

"There's no communication trenches down that away, boyo," said Taff, "just a hell of a lot o' wounded. Where's the wee one?"

The flashes of exploding shells illuminated the concerned eyes of the sappers as Johnny nodded at the tunnel entrance. In the magic of the moment the chaos and noise ceased and the men rushed forward into the black maw of the earth to find Solly. The lighting of a match broke the darkness. Kinney held the match and grunted.

"Gi' us a feckin' candle, Taff! We cannae see yon feckin' wee yin."

Taff pulled a candle from his bullet pouch and touched it to the match. The grimy faces would frighten a banshee in this eerie light but the baby's eyes were alight with glee. Johnny appeared amongst the grinning faces and gave an exaggerated cough. A big man, the Sergeant Major of the King's Liverpool Regiment, followed him. All but Solly stood up to face him and hid the baby from his view. The Sergeant Major thrust out his hand for Johnny to shake.

"We've lost thee; ye are to make your way back t' rear echelon."

He heartily grabbed all of the sapper's hands in turn, except Solly's whom he did not see holding the baby.

"Many more of my young soldiers would be dead but for t' Royal Engineers, I cannot thank thee enough. I hope ye don't mind me reporting thy valour to my CO for the lives ye saved today?"

Johnny and the sappers simply beamed smiles at him hoping he would go away so they could see the baby.

"That's very kind of thee, sir, but we'll 'ave a brew afore we go. Tha' knows, wet t' whistle while we can, which reminds me. How did Mr Anderson get on?"

The Sergeant Major's face dropped with sadness.

"Oh, Christ almighty. He died blowin' that bloody whistle. Standin' there, all six feet fuckin' odd of 'im, blowin' for all he was worth. So sad, a young bloke like that, this fuckin' war."

Taff caught Johnny's eye with a fuck him expression.

"My sentiment too, sir," said Johnny, "but I suspect things'd be different if generals and politicians shared these trenches wi' us."

The Sergeant Major patted Johnny's shoulder and disappeared into the whiz-bang night to tend to his wounded and frightened young soldiers along this sector of the front, talking to himself as he went.

In the mouth of the tunnel the sappers busied themselves preparing a meal and hot drinks. They each made a contribution that worked like clockwork while all around them in the nearby trench was pandemonium. Solly propped the nosebag so the baby was comfortable and deftly rolled a ciggie. He called to nobody in particular.

"Warm some tinned milk for t' baby."

Yiggs and Tat fussed about a little camping stove with mess tins and mugs, as Brummie opened a tin of bully beef and Andy pulled out hardtack biscuits from one of his bullet pouches. Seemingly an invisible wall separated chaos from the sappers and the trench warfare just a few feet away as they sat or crouched in a protective ring around the baby, all in a position to see the little pink face in the candle light and glowing ciggies as they ate and smoked. Johnny looked at the faces of his men, each face a roadmap of the most sustained onslaught on the human psyche, each of them desensitised to the brutal everyday loss of life. Looking at them he felt the love, the trust, the dependency on each other as warriors. Just then the saying brothers in arms was tangible. He knew he was in safe hands and they knew they were in his safe hands. He looked at his watch.

"Ten minutes an' we're off."

Yiggs looked at Solly.

"Thee's already off" he said, "see ye don't pass yer lice onto t' little fella."

Andy joined in.

"Nah, 'es a feckin' Jew; 'e'll gi' feck all away. He even wakes up t' see if 'es lost any feckin' sleep."

"Bollocks, haggis brain, you…" Solly replied.

"Leave ma family emblem ootta this, ye…"

"Sithee," said Tat, "what might that be, bollocks or haggis?"

"Who pulled thy feckin' chain?" asked Kinney.

The banter rolled on as they prepared to move out, until Johnny spoke.

"Solly, ye can be Gunga Din for t' baby until we get back. Give 'im t' medics, the nurses'll look after 'im. We 'ave a hole to dig."

"Bloody hell," said Taff, "ye must have read Kipling to mention Gunga Din."

"Methinks every bugger's read Gunga Din. We 'ad t' read it an' learn it in our school an' t' last line'll live wi' me always," said Johnny.

"What's that?" asked Taff.

"Thee's a better man than I am, Gunga Din!" quoted Johnny, "I thought ye would 'ave known that? Bloody ignorant Welsh."

"You're a better man than I am, Gunga Din!" quoted Taff, "I do bloody know it. I'll tell thee word for bloody word later."

"I look forward t' thee entertainin' lads down t' 'ole when we gets there."

The sappers disappeared along the dark tunnel shouting fresh banter and laughter, surreal amidst the earth-shaking sounds of war. The banter ended as soon as they exited the tunnel to trudge across acres and acres of the bloody battlefield. The dead were everywhere, cut to pieces with shrapnel and bullets, limbless torsos, young heads with sightless eyes gazed at the sky. Faces hideously scarred, yet others seemingly untouched stared blankly at the coming dawn. The sappers were seemingly superhuman not to be affected by this often recurring journey through the desecration of human life, caused by the unworthy, unthinking, shameless armchair warriors, the initiators of this dreadful war.

In the hectic medic's area of rear echelon known as the Casualty Clearing Area hundreds of wounded awaited treatment for their wounds. Stretcher-bearers laid out the dead in rows as far as the poor light of dawn allowed eyes to see, not quite equally as abhorrent as being on the battlefield. Solly and Allballs approached a blood-spattered nurse, one of the few females treating the wounded, as she knelt to adjust the dressing on a young man's stump, where his leg used to be. She looked up at Solly as he pulled the nosebag from his shoulder and put it down into her free arm and pulled away the cloth to reveal the tiny captivating pink face. The nurse was taken completely by surprise at such a sight here in Satan's abattoir, as she eased the baby out of the nosebag and hummed a tune.

"He's French, an' 'e's an orphan," said Solly. "Our Staff Sergeant, Johnny Gordon, nearly died savin' 'im in no man's land. Look after 'im will ye?"

Allballs tugged Solly away and stumbled amongst the wounded laid out in seemingly endless rows. Mumbling and moans of pain emitted from bloody ragged bundles of humanity. Allballs was concerned about Solly.

"Sithee, Solly, let's not dally 'ere. Fair plays on my fragile mind, tha' knows. Yon baby'll be safe now."

The lusty infantile cry of the baby momentarily silenced the murmuring of the wounded as the nurse carried him to a tent. Solly's granite face crumbled under the pressure of primal pity and frustration. Tears escaped, cutting channels through his facial grime as an uncontrollable sob escaped his breast. With an enormous effort of will Solly conquered his fleeting loss of stoical endurance and barged into Allballs throwing his arm around his shoulder like old pals do and off they went between the lines of dying men, both sappers with tears in their eyes as they strolled along trying like hell to be cheerful.

"Down t' 'ole is better 'n goin' o'er t' fuckin' top," said Solly.

"Aye, but sithee," said Allballs, "it's got its moments. Remember Kinney fallin' down t' Glory Hole shaft and Johnny shouted, have ye broken anything?"

118

"There's na much ta feckin' break doon 'ere," Kinney shouted back.

The pair of warriors chuckled at the memory but only for a moment as their faces masked the hidden fear of tunnelling under enemy lines.

There was nothing enjoyable about a battlefield, but in the HQ area of rear echelon there was an ablutions tent where men could shower and receive fresh clothes like socks and underwear. Johnny and his men lined up ready to enter the tent that had steam pouring out of every hole and opening in the canvas. Someone shouted and the queue of grimy men stripped naked and entered the delousing section before showering and foot inspections. They eased forward each carrying his bundle of clothes to where Chinese labourers stirred a line of steaming vats full of boiling water ready to kill the lice. In the thick fog of steam each man thrust his bundle of clothes into his designated vat and the Chinese man swiftly submersed it, boiling the lice. The men looked on from the nearby showers and Brummie could not resist it.

"Chuck an egg in it Chinky. We'll 'ave egg flied lice fer tea."

The men laughed, as did the Chinese, and them chattering in Mandarin just made it funnier. The men collected their clothing as they came out of the massive mangle still hot and steaming. Cautiously shuffling forward on wooden duckboards the men took their places seated on a long bench, with feet outstretched in front of them as a medic inspected each foot in turn and doused it with medication. All done the men paired off to perform their own delousing drill. One held a lit candle as the other passed the seams of their clothing over the flame. They smiled as they heard the lice popping like Chinese crackers. All done Johnny gathered his men.

"Right, listen in. We report to Requiem shaft tonight so let's get some hot grub an' a kip. We're goin' to need it. Hellfire Jack is in charge tonight so it'll be tough."

The men finished dressing in silence. Some pulled on fresh socks, others pulled on boots over bare feet. Their hard faces could not quite hide the trepidation of what was to come. The arrival of a small Chinese man carrying a large tray with steaming mugs and thick white bread piled high on it started the banter.

"Fuckin' 'ell, 'ow did 'e do that?" asked Yiggs.

"Do what?" asked Tat.

"Bring that food all t' way across 'ere wi' his eyes shut," replied Yiggs.

Though he saw that the penny had not dropped for everyone he made no further comment as they all tucked into the grub. That day the men slept as best they could in a demolished cowshed but being sappers they would have slept on a bed of nails, so no sweat. Then they gathered in the darkness and waited in the shadow of the sandbag wall revetment[19] that was the entrance to the Requiem Shaft tunnel. To the east and west of the shaft were the front line trenches full of British infantrymen. Star shells lit the sky as exploding shells and the zip of sniper fire made up the tapestry of the night sky.

The shaft entrance was covered with a tarpaulin sheet, which acted as a blackout cover. Further inside was another tarpaulin sheet, the secondary blackout. Men who were about to leave the tunnel gathered between the two tarpaulin sheets before exiting without shedding any light. These entrances were top secret and great care was taken to prevent their discovery by aircraft and enemy raiding squads. Consequently strict entry and exit drills were performed at each shift change. A group of men exited, their faces bereft of any recognisable expression - no banter, just an atmospheric sense of relief to be out of hell. Johnny was somewhat dismayed with his timing. He should have got here two or three minutes later.

"Oh fuck it let's get in there now an' thank thy lucky stars ye're not wi' t' fuckin' infantry."

Johnny ushered his men forward through the first tarp and on through the second to enter the hell of subterranean warfare. A heightened sense of awareness now descended over the hushed

---

[19] revetment - in military engineering these are structures, again sloped, formed to secure an area from artillery, bombing, or stored explosives

sappers. With faces steel-cut they silently descended the ladders of the fabricated steel shaft down to the main gallery and picked up the required tools. All set and ready to go they stood silently. Waiting. Waiting. A fearsome energy was in the air, a mix of trepidation and vigour felt by everyone about to enter the bowels of the earth through tiny tunnels - these often collapsed and killed many sappers.

Out of the gloom loomed Hellfire Jack, eyes glittering in the poor light of paraffin lamps and candles recessed into the walls and hanging from wooden pit props. Even in the dismal dangerous surroundings of the gallery he looked truly handsome, dashing and totally ruthless.

"Good evening, gentlemen," said Hellfire Jack. "Welcome to my parlour. It is a new parlour and you are about to extend it..." he pointed to his feet, "that away." He looked into each face as he spoke, "Silent digging, which means clay kicking all night. No coughing or sneezing and no talking. You will see at the end of this main gallery two tunnels, one to the left and the other... obviously. You will be working the West Wing, which is the left tunnel, the East Wing being the right tunnel."

He looked into Johnny's face and clasped his shoulder.

"Staff Sergeant Gordon here has a reputation to keep, as does Sergeant Dupree. So I know the Bosch will not hear us tonight, or any other bloody night, will they, sappers?"

Not a sound, as each man gawped into his meaningful eyes. Johnny braced himself and asked.

"I am a man short, sir. Billy Nolan hasn't yet been replaced."

Hellfire Jack turned to Taff. Their eyes met.

"Sergeant Dupree will take Billy's place. That right, Taff?"

"Too bloody true, boyo... er, I mean Colonel, sir, sorry 'bout that."

The men stifled their giggles as they picked up their tools and rifles and lined up ready to move into the gloom. Hellfire Jack had something to say about that.

"Leave your weapons here. Staff's pistol will suffice for now. The Bosch have not detected us yet and I am relying on you to keep it that way." He then spoke in mock Shakespearian, "Follow me in the name of the King. King George, who will one day hear of your exploits in the terrible underground world of tunnel warfare beneath the poppy fields of France."

With Hellfire Jack leading, they silently shuffled along the murky tunnel on a downward gradient until the last head disappeared from view. The sappers arrived at the bottom of the gradient to see a vast dugout containing thousands of setts, sandbags, rubber wheeled trolleys and the rails they ran on. Walking cautiously through groups of men busy pushing and pulling trolleys along a narrow-gauge railway line that disappeared into another tunnel, the sappers saw the usual Chinese labour gangs responsible for dealing with the spoils of the dig. Apart from heavy breathing the place was silent. Ahead of the sappers the rail track split into two. One track disappeared into a hole bearing a hand written sign above the entrance West Wing and the adjacent hole East Wing just a few feet away. The men halted with a hiss from Hellfire Jack.

"Right, you are all familiar with how the system works. Three men. A kicker, a bagger and a trammer normally work one-hour shifts but you can do two hours on and two hours off if you prefer it. But you will do an eight-hour dig. The quartermaster keeps hot food and drink on the go so help yourselves between shifts. The QM is Warrant Officer Connor, Jim Connor, I'm sure you all know him." He stepped back, saluted and whispered, "Right, get on with it."

He silently disappeared whence he came through the darkness, as Johnny took charge of his men again.

"Taff, thee take Solly, Yiggs an' Allballs. I'll follow ye in a minute." Johnny turned to the others, "The rest of ye go an' find t' way around this dump an' see where everything is. Prepare a kip[20] for all of us an' we'll do a one-hour shift 'til we see the conditions down there. I'm off t' find Jim Connor."

---

[20] kip - somewhere to rest

Taff and his crew loaded a trolley with setts and sandbags and disappeared into the hole of the West Wing pushing the trolley ahead of them, as the others started their recce of the compound and vanished amongst stacks of mining paraphernalia.

In the far corner of the compound was a shed with light shining through the open door. Johnny walked into a manly hug and shoulder slapping with Jim Connor.

"Fuckin' 'ell, Johnny, I knew ye was comin' but not so soon. Sorry to hear about Billy Nolan, his Ma'll be in bits, poor woman."

"Oh aye, it's worse when tha knows t' family. She's my fuckin' mother-in-law. My missus'll be in bits too. I'll write to her shortly. Fuckin' war. Anyway what about this tunnel? And is the Bosch active around 'ere?"

Jim poured Johnny a cup of tea and offered a ciggie and frowned.

"The tunnel's a fuckin' long un an' Fritz was ere before us, so aye, Fritz is diggin' away like fuck, but he ain't heard us yet."

Johnny sipped the hot tea and put it down on the wooden table.

"Too fuckin' hot, I'll check on my lads an' be back in a minute. Oh, where are t' friends?"

Jim Connor pointed over Johnny's shoulder.

"O'er yonder, in t' dark corner, but I doubt thee'll need 'em. We've had no gas in this sector, yet."

Johnny slunk out of the shed and headed for the dark corner where he could hear the friends chirping. Reaching up he took a small cage housing a single bird from the stack. Bringing it back into the light he saw it was a robin, not the usual canary familiar to all miners.

"Hello Mister Robin, fancy meetin' thee here. I'll set thee free when we come out o' t' hole."

Hiding the bird in his tunic he forgot the hot tea and headed straight for the West Wing tunnel. Bent double in the tunnel he checked the setts as he crept down the gradient, deeper into the bowels of the earth where the roof height diminished to trolley height. Out of the murky light came a loaded trolley. Johnny quickly squeezed into a recess cut into the tunnel wall and waited for it to pass. Noiselessly the trolley bypassed Johnny and stopped as Taff saw Johnny in the alcove. Taff gesticulated for Johnny to follow him back out, mouthing the word Jerry. They headed back up the gradient to the compound where the trolley was passed to a Chinese labourer who silently disappeared with it along the tunnel. Turning to Johnny, Taff whispered in his ear.

"I can hear Jerry diggin' t' left of our gallery. They might breach our wall. I need a pistol."

Johnny whispered back into Taff's ear as he pulled out his pistol.

"Take mine. I'll get a geophone from Jim Connor an' be wi' thee shortly."

Taff pushed an empty trolley silently down the gradient as Johnny headed for the office. His silent entry made Jim Connor jump.

"What the fuck! Why're ye fuckin' creepin' about? Givin' me the fuckin' jitters. Whassup?"

"I need a geophone, now Jim, down t' West hole. My men can hear Jerry scrapin' around near our face."

"Fuck, fuck! Are ye fuckin' sure? We ain't heard a squeak from Jerry since we started these galleries."

"Well 'es fuckin' squeakin' now. When Taff says it's Jerry, it's fuckin' Jerry. So gimme t' fuckin' geophone so we can track 'im."

Jim pulled open a huge cupboard and stood back.

"Take yer pick, Johnny."

Johnny scanned the cupboard, reached in and lifted out a box the size of a biscuit tin. He also grabbed a stethoscope.

"Lend me thy pistol just in case they break through, there's no room for rifles down there."

Jim pulled his pistol from the holster hanging on the door.

"It's loaded an' ye'd best take some grenades. I'll get t' news t' Hellfire Jack. He'll be back 'ere like a ragin' fuckin' bull."

"Just hope he's got bullets in that fuckin' posh pistol of his? I've got a bad feelin' about this job," said Johnny.

"Oh, he's got bullets all right. I've seen him use that posh pistol. He's no fuckin' dandelion, Johnny. I reckons he pisses sulphuric acid and thee can rely on Hellfire Jack, he didn't get that name for bible thumping, tha knows."

Johnny stuffed grenades into his tunic pockets and headed for the West Wing tunnel and the clay face where his men were on their knees silently listening to sounds of digging and scraping. Crawling on all fours, Johnny silently approached his men. They looked on as he deftly placed grenades into a recess cut into the sidewall where a candle flickered. Reaching into his tunic he pulled out the tiny cage with the robin inside and gently placed it next to the grenades. The men had their ears cocked, listening to the sounds of voices speaking in German. Allballs raised his hand indicating five Germans digging west of them, possibly three or four feet below. Johnny responded by passing the geophone to Taff and using the stethoscope on the clay sidewall of the tunnel as Taff set up the geophone. With earpieces in place Taff adjusted the listening discs and immediately pointed west at a downward angle. Johnny passed the stethoscope to Allballs and indicated for him to stay with Solly and Yiggs, listening.

Johnny and Taff then left, crawling on all fours and headed for the shed where they met Jim Connor and Hellfire Jack. A brew was on the go so Jim poured four cups of tea as Hellfire Jack rolled out a drawing on the table.

"Jolly bad show Jerry showing up on our patch. What have you got?"

"About four feet down an' t' west of our face. Jerry is diggin' towards us. He'll be abreast of us in a couple of hours, but I reckon 'e'll miss by a foot or two," said Johnny.

"Bloody hell!" said Jack. "Prepare for the worst. Take weapons and grenades in case they break through. If they do, you must kill them all and collapse their gallery before they can counter attack."

"They must think they're alone down there, sir," said Taff, "the banging and chatter is too loud for them to think otherwise. They don't know we are here else they'd be more careful."

"I hope you are right, Sergeant Dupree," said Hellfire Jack, "but I am sure you will kill them all anyway. What?"

Poking the drawing with his finger Hellfire Jack snorted.

"He's obviously heading for the big crater just in front of our lines, which means his tunnel is meant to move troops forward, safe from our artillery shells. Bloody hell! Jerry must be attacking all along the salient,[21] probably this week."

The men looked at each other stone-faced. Fucking hell. Johnny and Taff took their leave and headed for the West Wing tunnel. Crawling on hands and knees towards his men, Johnny could hear the Germans even before he reached his men. Soundlessly, the five men crouched in the confined space of the tunnel. Sweat ran down each face as the tension increased. Their eyes smarted as the sweat leaked into them. Their hearts pounded so hard as to be heard in their tiny clay coffin.

A sudden tweet from the robin sounded like a trumpet fanfare in the tense silence, which made them all jump with fright. Fuck!

The bird looked straight at Johnny. Tweet!

The German digging stopped. Absolute silence, the sappers' faces cut like the clay they dug. Eyes flashed in the flickering candlelight as Johnny slowly reached up and gently grasped the tiny cage to slowly bring it down but not without dislodging a grenade.

In the German gallery the mining crew consisted of eight miners and an officer. They stood in silence, listening, holding their breath. Two men at the face held picks, two men just behind them held spades, two men behind them held sandbags and two men behind them loaded bags onto a trolley. They all stood stock still, listening.

The German tunnel was big enough to stand in and their officer was standing with his finger to his mouth shushing them to silence, his face daring them to make a sound - as if they would. They all stood there motionless, silent. Then they heard someone coming

---

21 salient - also known as a bulge, is a battlefield feature that projects into enemy territory. The salient is surrounded by the enemy on multiple sides, making the troops occupying the salient vulnerable

along their tunnel towards them whistling a tune so the officer crept away from his men to silence the whistler.

In the West Wing tunnel the men helplessly looked at the grenade falling from the ledge. It hit a spade with a metallic clang as Johnny dropped the bird in his effort to catch the grenade. He heard a baby cry and froze stock-still. So Taff bent forward instead to catch the grenade and the robin tweeted loudly as you would expect it to.

The pointed end of a pick came crashing through the clay wall straight into Taff's eye and through to his brain, killing him instantly as they all fell through the collapsing wall down into the German gallery.

Johnny, on one knee started shooting the German miners. In the chaos of killing, Solly tossed a grenade after the escaping officer and two of his men. They died in the blast. Using Taff's pistol, Yiggs shot the fleeing Germans trying to escape. He killed them all and then strolled around and shot each in the head just to make sure. In the haze of cordite fumes they quickly assessed the situation. The silence was oppressive as Johnny, on one knee, contemplated the smoking muzzle of his pistol. His bitter brooding expression jolted his men.

"Sithee, Staff, we 's all goin' to miss 'im," said Allballs.

"Aye," said Yiggs, "but not as much as…"

"Shhh," said Johnny.

He handed his pistol to Solly with a box of ammo from his bullet pouch. With hand signals and nods the sappers took up post along the tunnel where the dead German officer lay. Turning to the rubble and the twisted body of Taff, he knelt and pulled out the pick from Taff's head.

"Ye shoulda gone 'ome t' Wales boyo when ye had the chance."

There was a moment of deep grief as Taff's one open eye paled over as though his soul was saying goodbye. A single tear cut a crease through the muck on Johnny's face. A noise behind him made him turn to see Jim Connor holding a couple of pistols in outstretched hands toward him.

"Here, take these, they're loaded. I've got a drum of ammonal in the trolley. Thee'll have to blow this Jerry hole sharpish. We heard the shootin' up top so Jerry'll be investigating any minute now. What the fuck 'appened?"

Johnny took the weapons and placed them on the ground.

"Jerry heard us an' pulled our tunnel wall into theirs. Now I've lost Taff, the best soldier I…"

"Jerry fuckin' heard you!" Jim Connor exploded. "Don't let fuckin' Hellfire Jack hear that. This tunnel is key to his big plan an' thy reputation will be dog shit if thee open's gob about Jerry findin' ye, an' make sure thy men knows what to say if asked."

"His big plan! We've been diggin' out big plans fer over a year an' many good men died fer it. Yon big planners should be down 'ere wi' us. Shit on their fuckin' plans."

"Aye, I agree," said Jim, "but I'm tellin' 'im that Jerry blundered into our tunnel an' you lot killed 'em all, an' ye best back me up."

"All right Jim. I'll tell my men t' same. Thee's a good pal, Jim. Now I must get Taff t' fresh air."

"Not before we set this drum o' ammonal ready t' blow, ye ain't."

Jim Connor wrestled the fifty-pound drum of explosive out of his tunnel into Johnny's arms in the German tunnel.

"We need more than this t' block it proper, plenty more," said Johnny.

"I know that," said Jim, "but we haven't the fuckin' time. Ye fix it ready t' blow while I go back for more. One's better 'n nowt. If Jerry attacks blow it."

Jim Connor disappeared back along the tunnel as Johnny rolled the drum to where the three sappers were alert and prepared for a counter attack.

"Too quiet for my liking, Staff. Should've had a response by now," Solly whispered.

"Aye," said Yiggs, "they might have adjoining tunnels like we have and they're mining it ready to bury us."

"Shut up, ye daft bat," said Johnny, "put t' primer on this ready to blow an' cut t' safety fuse fer a one-minute burn."

"One fuckin' minute!" exclaimed Allballs. "Look how far we have to run?"

"Yer a fuckin' ferret, Allballs,'" said Johnny, "ye'll be up yon hole like a fuckin' rat up a spout. Fuckin' cut it."

Hearing a noise behind him, Johnny went back to the breach where Kinney, Brummie and Tat, each with a drum of Ammonal, were passing them down into the German tunnel.

"Right," said Johnny, "ye, Tat, roll 'em over t' t'others an' ye two get Taff up top an' come back wi' more ammonal."

Tat got on with it and Johnny helped him while Kinney and Brummie grunted with the effort of squeezing Taff back through the breach. Silently the sappers placed the charge and fitted the primer, detonator and safety fuse ready to blow. Each of them knew the predicament they were in, but uncaring Solly broke the silence with a magnificent trumpeting fart, which started the giggles.

"If Jerry comes now we's all fucked cos Taff is blockin' our escape."

Johnny sniffed the air noisily and stage whispers.

"If Jerry comes now, he'll think we's usin' fuckin' mustard gas," Johnny pointed to the breach, "Get over there an' get 'im out. I'll stay 'ere while ye lot bring back a drum o' Ammonal each. Go on, fuck off."

The sappers crept back to the breach and helped the others to move the dead Taff, doing their best not to make a sound.

*

Many miles away and doing the exact opposite, was Cathryn, Taff's wife, moaning in ecstasy as she lay on Beryl's bed, semi naked wearing her new silk shift and French satin camiknickers, while Beryl licked the satin with her tongue into her slit.

CHAPTER SEVEN

Just a day after her own solo sexual awakening Beryl called round to Taff's house on the pretence of having a cup of tea and a chat. Cathryn was truly delighted that her friend had called and gladly chucked the mop and bucket into the back yard. She made a pot of tea and pulled fresh scones out of the range oven.

"It is so nice of ye to come an' see me. I've seen no one this week. What 'ave ye been up to? C'mon, tuck in, here's butter n' jam, ne'er mind t' waistline, there's no strong man's hands to grab it, is there?" Cathryn said, giggling.

"Aye, lass, tha's right there's, no strong men," Beryl replied.

Cathryn suddenly realised how well groomed and made-up Beryl was. She looked fresh and beautiful - her cosmetics applied just so, not for a man, for this was before noon.

"Are ye going shopping to Liverpool or Manchester? Tha's lookin' as though tha's goin' somewhere special for an interview for a job or something?" asked Cathryn.

"I'm goin' to a little old bookshop I know in Widnes," said Beryl, as she fumbled out the book that enlightened her and put it on the table. "I'm goin' for more of this because the loneliness was making me suicidal and I don't need a man now that I've found this and discovered myself."

Slightly shocked, Cathryn could see her best friend blushing but somehow confident with a hint of serenity about her. She leant across to take the book but Beryl pulled it back.

"Read it when I've gone. The bookkeeper's wife told me she gets her ladies books from overseas, mainly from France and Persia, translated into English and with exquisite illustrations. But now ye can give me the local gossip. What's this about Ruth an' that twat, Albert Jennings?"

Later that day Beryl returned from Widnes with her new books, two of them hardbacks. She placed her bag on the table and dashed upstairs to change her clothes. She came back down and gave the fire a poke and banked it up with more coal, made a pot of tea and buttered a couple of Cathryn's scones. At last, she thought, I can relax and clear my mind of the shite of this miserable fucking dump. Biting into a thickly buttered scone and sipping her tea, choosing which book to read was the best moment of her day up until then. Better moments lay ahead inside the books.

It was teatime in Cathryn's house and she ladled a bowl of beef bone broth from the stockpot on the range. After filtering it through muslin cloth it looked just like a savoury consommé, which she ate with her own baked bread and butter. She was careful not to drip any onto the book she could not put down. She had mixed feelings about it and was struggling with her conscience, but her conscience was losing because she was most certainly aroused and wondered why Beryl, her very modern and confident best friend, had planted this particular seed on her.

She closed the book and ate her meal and imagined herself and Beryl as being the two classy French girls in the drawings. The more she thought about it the more eroticism played in her mind. Cathryn wondered what it would be like to kiss another woman but when she visualised Beryl's lovely lips and imagined the brushing of lips and the tender embrace and the touching of breasts, she succumbed to the notion of female loving – at least until the men come home.

Her mind made up she decided to visit Beryl that night. She checked the fire in the range and secured the fireguard in front of it after first pouring the hot water in the kettle into an enamel bowl in which she washed herself, taking care with her flannel to clean her private parts. She did this in front of the fire before going upstairs to find her best lingerie. Feeling excited but doubtful, she took another look at the book at the page with the exquisite drawing of the two French ladies and with that image in mind she left home to stride confidently to Beryl's house.

The light knocks on the door made Beryl jump and quickly close the book on the table and pull her bathrobe tight around her, holding her breath, which she slowly exhaled as she heard the lilting Welsh voice.

"'Tis only me Bee. Are ye there?"

"Coming, Cathryn," she unbolted the door and let her in. "Give me your coat. Sit at t' table, I'll get another glass. Ye likes a drop o' sherry?"

Cathryn handed her the coat and their hands touched momentarily. Their eyes met and the coat fell away as a spontaneous reaction occurred between them and, for the first time in years of knowing each other, they embraced. Their emotions made them swoon with the release of the tensions they suddenly realised were not really there anyway. A new happiness occurred between them and like a couple of school girls they held hands and strolled to the table where lay the initiators of this exciting liaison, beautifully written and illustrated pornography in books from Persia.

"I bought two new books today. I looked at several but found it difficult to choose between them," said Beryl. "So I told the lady I should return in a week or so to buy two more and she told me I can exchange them for a smaller fee if they're not damaged. So I thought we could go together next time and spend t' day shopping."

"Oh, how thoughtful of thee; I'd love t' go shoppin' wi' thee, I need a change of scenery," said Cathryn. "I suppose nobody else knows about these books?"

"I wouldn't tell anybody the time in this dump," Beryl replied, her heart beating happily.

"But you told me," said Cathryn.

Looking intently into each other's eyes, Beryl whispered.

"I love thee, an' I can see thee loves me so we can say anything to each other an' I don't care if I never speak to another soul in this place."

Their hands moved simultaneously across the table to entwine fingers lovingly, and continued gazing into each other's eyes their love blossomed with each meaningful moment.

"Sherry or bed?" asked Beryl.

"I'm stayin' t' night," replied Cathryn, "so sherry please. A large one."

They sat in front of the fire, which provided just enough light and atmosphere for lovers, chatting and gazing into each other's eyes when they were not looking into the fire. Their talk was of themselves, not a word about the war or men or about the place in which they lived, but occasionally touching on the contents of the books. They did not stay up drinking sherry for long.

"Bedtime," said Beryl, and they both got up from their chairs and embraced. "I'll get some water to take up. Thee go on up, there's a candle lightin' t' way at top t' stairs and another in t' bedroom."

Cathryn climbed the stairs in candlelight, which heightened the excitement with every step. She entered the bedroom and caught her breath as she saw the large bed in the flickering candlelight with the sheets turned down ready for climbing in. She shrugged off the bathrobe that Beryl gave her and started to pull down her satin knickers.

"Leave them on. I will enjoy taking those off," said Beryl, as she entered the bedroom, "and then thee can take mine off."

Cathryn pulled her knickers back up and as her slip dropped back into place Beryl embraced her slowly and tenderly so that their breasts touched. The exciting emotions flowed rapidly through both of them as their nipples met and could be felt through the flimsy material of their lingerie. They kissed and their tongues touched, as did their mons pubis causing feelings of desire neither woman had ever experienced, but which felt so wonderful. This seemed natural and was, for some as yet unknown reason, meant to happen.

That unknown reason was actually taking root right now beneath the poppy fields of France, in the German underground tunnels along the Western Front.

CHAPTER EIGHT

In the German underground HQ the opulence displayed the months of occupation with its carpets and polished wooden furniture, but even more so, by the splendid uniforms of the officers with their shiny boots.

On the walls were charts with drawings of galleries all along the German front line - the result of months of digging. A captain with a livid duelling scar on his left cheek was pointing his swagger stick at a dotted line on the wall chart as a group of dirty miners looked on. Hauptmann (Captain) Ernst Hoffman, immaculate in his fitted tunic and highly polished boots, briefed his men.

"The English are here at the face of the main gallery... correct, Private Scorzeny?" he pointed his stick at a dirty little man who nodded affirmatively. "And they have only pistols and grenades, yes?"

Private Scorzeny shifted his weight uneasily from one foot to the other.

"I heard two pistols and one grenade as I approached the face," he said. "They did not see me coming so I crept back into the shadows and returned here to report the presence of the enemy, sir."

"You didn't think to return fire?"

"My pick doesn't have a trigger so I thought it prudent to report it, sir."

The men stifled their giggles but not quickly enough for the likes of Ernst Hoffman, a typical Prussian martinet. He gave Scorzeny an icy glare.

"Today I am to execute three men for cowardice in the face of the enemy. You, Scorzeny, are in that grey area where I haven't yet made up my mind for you to be the fourth. I think it prudent for you to exhibit much courage today."

The men shifted uncomfortably but spoke not a word. Their hard, grimy faces portrayed the harshness of much time spent

134

digging beneath the fields of France and Flanders. A fact that Ernst Hoffman could not care less about, as he constantly flaunted his patrician airs and superior status over these Bavarian miners.

Turning back to the wall chart he again prodded the dotted line. Alternately pointing at adjacent lines on the chart, he turned quickly, eyeballing the men.

"These two tunnels were dug months ago and if the Englanders are here," pointing his stick, "we can use the eastern tunnel to mine their main gallery, which must be here," again pointing his stick. "We know this tunnel is deeper than theirs so we can dig beneath them starting a tunnel at right angles here and place a charge big enough to completely wreck their plans."

His icy blue eyes scanned the men and stopped at the two big men standing to the right of the miners.

"Sergeant Braun and Corporal Stein, carry out this task immediately."

Sergeant Braun, aged about forty, was obviously a tough guy sporting a broken nose and many scars around his face, stood to attention and shouted.

"Jawohl, Herr Hauptmann!"

Corporal Stein, athletic and just a few years younger than Sergeant Braun, was not so eager but spoke calmly.

"Herr Hauptmann, will you be picking the exact place to start work?"

The men felt the instant change in demeanour, as this innocent question was a touché moment for the earlier cowardice slant. It was difficult to see the innocuous expression on Corporal Stein's face through the layers of muck, but artfully, it was there and Hauptmann Hoffman smarted.

"Would you have me take you by the hand, Corporal Stein? Your place of work is down there amongst the worms, safe from enemy snipers and artillery shells. Any more stupid remarks and you will be a private up here in the trenches. Get out!"

The men exited the HQ, unable to hide their smirks.

In the West Wing tunnel, Kinney pulled as Brummie pushed the dead Taff onto a flat trolley but the going was slow in such a confined space. Kinney crawled backwards on all fours up the gradient using Taff's webbing belt clamped in his teeth as the towrope. Brummie pushed Taff's boots at the other end. The sweat poured from them as they emerged into the larger gallery where they could stand upright. Jim Connor waited for them where Chinese labourers soundlessly placed drums of ammonal ready to send to Johnny on the trolley. Gently the Chinese crew picked up Taff's body and silently disappeared along the gallery. The sappers quietly bade their brother in arms a heartfelt farewell.

"But this war waits for no man," Jim Connor stage whispered, "fuckin' move! Get these down to Johnny smartish and come back for more. Tell 'im Hellfire Jack is on his way an' he's not happy."

Jim Connor followed after the Chinese and Taff's body as the sappers loaded the trolley and silently took it down to the breach in the wall. Down there everything ran like clockwork as sappers moved to and fro with drums of ammonal and ever more arriving to feed the growing bomb. Soon an impressive stack of explosives blocked the entire tunnel except for an observation gap at the side. The initiation set was primed and Johnny crimped the one-minute safety fuse to the detonator and inserted it into the primer ready to blow.

Johnny wore a concerned expression as Hellfire Jack approached and whispered.

"Without tamping[22], this charge may not be enough to collapse the gallery nor allow our men to escape the blast. As you well know the explosion will follow the path of least resistance."

"I know, sir. But we don't 'ave time t' tamp it. Jerry 'asn't been t' see us yet so I reckons 'e's gonna counterattack wi' a charge somewhere near us. I will leave one man 'ere to light the fuse while

---

[22] tamping - in blasting, the act or operation of filling up a blast-hole above the charge, typically to make it resistant to further compression

we clear the area and use t' geophone to check any movement nearby."

Hellfire Jack gave the thumbs up gesture and waved everyone out. Johnny gave Solly the fuse matches and whispered.

"I'll be back t' tell ye t' strike but, if Jerry comes afore me, ye strike it and get out fast."

In the deathly silence their eyes met - no fear just solid trust in each other. Fear would come soon enough for any man in that position.

Beneath the German front line in the tunnel Hauptmann Hoffman had designated as the relief tunnel, Sergeant Braun led his men along the eerie, poorly lit tunnel, which was big enough for men to be three abreast and to stand upright to enable mass movement of troops.

Corporal Stein used a pace stick to measure the distance required to put them abreast of their other tunnel. Silently he pushed a stake into the clay wall. The men, all carrying digging tools and rifles, stood aside as the two NCOs measured exactly where along the wall they should start digging. Using his bayonet Corporal Stein cut an arch shape into the timbered clay wall and beckoned the men to silently remove the wooden boards and pit props.

The first cut into the clay started the new attacking tunnel. The Germans' haste created a low level of noise as they dug into the earth and bagged it for removal. Not knowing about geophones the Germans assumed the British used the same methods of listening as they did, stethoscopes et cetera.

Not too far away, as the worm crawls, Hellfire Jack and Johnny were on all fours using a geophone in the West Wing tunnel compound, as Jim Connor looked about him at the motionless workforce all standing like statues, dead still. Looking at the geophone motion discs with their earphones on, Johnny and Hellfire Jack simultaneously pointed their fingers west at a downward angle in line with the floating needles in the motion discs of the geophone.

"They have just started their attack tunnel, over there, to come beneath us," said Hellfire Jack.

Standing now, he gestured for everyone to be silent and stay put and beckoned Johnny to follow him.

"Over here, I have a deep communication tunnel. Hands and knees only I'm afraid, but enough for you to put in a bore hole charge to bring them down and their main gallery with them. Johnny, the race is on."

At the dark wall of the compound he pulled back a tarpaulin sheet, which was hiding a sandbag revetted[23] opening approximately three feet high by two feet wide and pitch black inside. The tarp fell back into place and Johnny went back to his men, still standing in silence, as Hellfire Jack climbed the Requiem shaft ladder to the fresh air of France and any other business.

Johnny instructed the men.

"Jim, 'ave ye got a borehole charge in t' store?"

"Aye lad, already primed an' ready to blow. Safety fuse or electric, got all t' bits 'ere when ye're ready," said Jim Connor.

"Good, give it t' Kinney." Looking at Kinney, "Check it an' bring it t' entrance, then get another one. The rest of ye get yer tools, a flat trolley an' sandbags. Jim, we need torches an' an auger for t' borehole charge an' yer Chinks can fill extra sandbags fer t' tampin'. Brummie, get t' geophone and come wi' me."

Silently they dispersed to start work. Brummie scooped up the geophone and followed Johnny to the tarp where he lit two torches then dropped to his knees and crawled into the communication tunnel. Johnny led the way on hands and knees down a steep gradient. Brummie lit the lamps in the recesses cut into the walls of the tunnel as he passed them. Reaching a point where an alcove was cut into the wall Johnny set up the geophone while Brummie lit more lamps nearby. In the oppressive silence and poor light,

---

[23] revet - face (a rampart, wall, etc.) with masonry, especially in fortification; sandbag and revetted trenches

138

Brummie watched as Johnny fitted the earpieces and started to listen. Johnny's face dribbled sweat onto his hands as he placed the motion discs first on the floor and then on the wall. Brummie's concerned face watched Johnny as he quickly took off the earpieces and gesticulated to move deeper.

Just a few yards further down the gradient. Johnny stopped and used the geophone again. Anxiously Brummie watched him place the motion discs on the wall and then on the roof of the tunnel. Quickly removing the earpieces he gave Brummie the thumbs up and whispered.

"You set up the trolley wi' sandbags an' make sure its secured wi' a good rope t' control t' descent. Put six bags on it an' Kinney can come down in front wi' t' auger[24]. Send Andy t' relieve Solly. Solly'll tell 'im what t' do. Thee's in charge up top. Send Solly down when 'e gets back 'ere. C'mon, tout de suite."

Brummie departed leaving Johnny listening to the enemy.

Beneath the German front line, seemingly oblivious to the noise they were making, the German miners dug ferociously into the hard earth face of their tunnel. The spoil was bagged and thrown back to a waiting trolley. Sergeant Braun and Corporal Stein stacked explosives onto another waiting trolley. Stein spoke without whispering.

"I hope this bang ends this fucking war. I swear I'll shoot that cunt, Hoffman if this goes on much longer."

"His resting place is down here in the shitty guts of France, just you wait and see," said Braun.

Stein's brooding face cracked into a grin.

"You crafty Bavarian yodeller, you've got a secret plan haven't you? I knew you were up to something to be quiet all this time. Our

---

[24] auger - a tool for boring holes or moving loose material

previous snotty bastard went missing. Herr Hauptmann Keller, been missing since Easter. Another Prussian prick just like this bastard."

Sergeant Braun grabbed Stein's neck and poked a bayonet into his gizzard, snarling quietly but frighteningly sincere.

"Ideas like that are dangerous, especially when you are already in your grave down here, you…"

Corporal Stein pushed him off rubbing his neck with one hand and a pistol in the other and snarled back.

"You too are in your grave if you touch me again. You need to ask for a weekend pass. You are beginning to look like a fucking mole instead of being my friend."

The German warriors simultaneously realised their strong bond was not worth breaking. They dropped their weapons and embraced with a strong hug and much backslapping.

"Let's give these fucking Tommys' a trip to the angels, just look at all these lovely fireworks," Sergeant Braun growled.

Private Scorzeny appeared pulling a trolley laden with sandbags full of spoil and wordlessly disappeared along the tunnel.

"Not long now, Herr Englander," Stein snarled.

Sergeant Braun's facial grime hid the fear within him as he knelt to look along the attack tunnel at his men beavering away at the clay face several yards into the cloying guts of France.

In the West Wing compound Brummie, Tat and Yiggs wrestled with a rope, feeding it through their hands, as the loaded trolley inched its way down the gradient towards Johnny and Kinney in the tiny communication tunnel. Jim Connor arrived with two Chinese labourers carrying a borehole charge. Gently they placed it next to another as Jim Connor put down a T handle shot blaster[25].

In the awful confined space of the tiny tunnel, with poor ventilation and light, Kinney used the earth auger drilling at an angle to bore beneath the Germans, who could now be heard digging not far away above them. The earth auger was difficult to use but

---

[25] shot blaster - plunger type

soundless. Johnny and Solly stacked sandbags, blocking their own tunnel on the downward side in order to form the tamping for their bomb. Johnny saw Kinney sweating profusely and struggling with the earth auger. Everything down here was said in whispers and hand signals.

Johnny prodded Kinney and whispered.

"Ye needs a break, 'ow much more?"

"Another foot, maybe eighteen inches. Clay's fuckin' solid."

"Right, get up top, send Allballs down wi' t' first torpedo. Go, fuck off."

Silently Kinney crawled away up the gradient as Johnny turned the earth auger churning the clay out of the hole, which was knackering in the foul air and confined space of the tunnel. Solly bagged the soil then they changed over, Solly turning the auger as Johnny bagged the spoil.

"Right, that'll do. Pull it out an' take it up top," said Johnny. "Where's fuckin' Allballs?"

"I'll get up top an' see, an' come back wi' a trolley fer t' auger," said Solly.

"Bring first torpedo wi yer… an' Allballs," ordered Johnny.

Just a minute or two later the trolley arrived with Allballs and Solly and a six feet long torpedo that weighed heavy and was difficult to push into the auger hole, bored to fit the torpedo in the tunnel wall. Grunting, pushing and sweating the sappers persevered in this confined space and finally slid it home so just the metal end cap was showing in the torchlight. Johnny unscrewed the end cap to reveal the initiation cavity, which he now cleaned off the grease from two brass segments with clips for electric detonation. In the centre of the cavity was a hole in which the safety fuse detonator was housed - so this device had a safety fuse option as well as electric detonation.

"Go get t' other torpedo. Bring it down nose first and bring t' blasting cable. Take t' auger back up wi' ye," Johnny whispered to Allballs.

Allballs lay flat on the trolley with the earth auger and tugged the rope. He noiselessly disappeared as the men up top pulled him up. Johnny used the geophone again and could hear German voices over the noise of the digging above him. He removed the earpieces and packed away the geophone.

"Don't need that anymore. Jerry's about ten feet away an' diggin' like hell. We'll wait 'til they stop an' start carryin' their explosives in," he whispered to Solly.

Allballs arrived with the second torpedo and a coil of wire.

"Go back an' get me two drums of ammonal, fuckin' quick," Johnny told him.

Allballs lay on the trolley, tugged the rope and off he went as Johnny and Solly wrestled with the second torpedo.

Beneath the German front line in the enemy relief tunnel Sergeant Braun beckoned his men to join him at the stack of explosives. The men crept out of the attack tunnel and sat with their sergeant, who gestured for them to light up their ciggies.

Corporal Stein entered the attack tunnel with his pace stick and in just a moment he went back out and whispered to Braun.

"Nearly there. Another two metres and we can load the explosives," he looked at the pile of sandbags, "tamping the charge will take half an hour and we need to fill more sandbags so we had better get cracking."

"Two minutes won't matter, here have a toke[26] on this. I got it from one of our Arab friends," said Braun, as the men grinned knowingly and Stein took a deep drag and grinned with them.

In the West Wing compound, Jim Connor supervised the loading of two drums of ammonal and ordered Allballs to descend backwards in front of the trolley to keep it steady on the gradient. Yiggs, Tat and Brummie controlled the descent with the rope until it

---

[26] toke - a pull on a cigarette or pipe, typically one containing cannabis

reached Johnny, then held fast while Allballs unloaded it. Johnny stopped him, shushing him to silence.

"They've stopped diggin'. Listen, quiet as t' grave now," he whispered.

Allballs looked at Solly's dirty face, the whites of his eyes looked bigger than usual as the sweat dripped off his chin.

"Sithee, Staff, did thee need to mention t' fuckin' grave?" Allballs whispered.

The palpable sense of fear increased as the noise of approaching Germans telegraphed through the overhead clay. The scraping sound of tools indicated further digging.

"Right, they've started diggin' again. Get that fuckin' ammonal in place here. Put a sandbag on each of them and place t' other torpedo on top," Johnny whispered.

Soundlessly the job was done as Johnny pared the electric cable ends and cut the wire to jury rig[27] the two torpedoes' brass clips in tandem, ensuring simultaneous detonation. Passing the coil of wire to Solly, he whispered.

"Take that up top and don't allow any fucker to connect t' shot blaster. Send Kinney to relieve Andy in the other tunnel an' tell Brummie we need more sandbags fer t' tamping."

Solly played out the wire as he left pushing it into the bottom edge of the tunnel so as not to get it tangled with feet or trolley wheels. Allballs fished out a roll of safety fuse from his bullet pouch and cut two arm's length pieces and handed it to Johnny, who crimped a detonator to each length and carefully inserted each of them into both of the torpedo primer holes.

"If by any chance t' electric dets don't blow,' said Johnny, "ye can dash down 'ere an' light these safety fuses."

"Sithee, Staff,' said Allballs, "why do they call it safety fuse?"

Johnny grinned at the gallows humour as the sandbags arrived. They laid the safety fuses next to the electric cable, trapping them so

---

[27] jury rig - makeshift repairs made with only the tools and materials at hand

they could be lit from the upward side. Silently they worked laying the sandbags from floor to roof forming a barrier for the back blast to be contained. The last of the sandbags was placed on the pile and Johnny whispered.

"Go tell Quartermaster Connor t' get all personnel out, Chinks, every fucker except my sappers."

Allballs crawled away up the incline then went to the shed and whispered his instructions to Jim Connor. In the complete silence of this massive dugout compound men slowly crept through the main gallery to the Requiem shaft ladder and up to the fresh air of France.

In the German relief tunnel eight bedraggled miners sat exhausted, wiping sweat and grime from their faces, as Private Scorzeny loaded heavy boxes of explosives onto a trolley and pulled it into the attack tunnel where Corporal Stein was preparing primers and paring cable ends for the detonation of this massive underground bomb. Scorzeny had to push the trolley through the tunnel on his knees because of its dimensions. When he reached Stein he could stand upright because they were inside the large, hewn out cavity, which was being filled with explosives. Puffing and panting Scorzeny started unloading the boxes. He accidentally dropped one, which gave a dull penetrating thud into the clay floor. In the dark confines of the camouflet his eyes bulged with fear and pain as Stein's big hands grabbed his scrawny throat and choked the gas out of him.

"You fucking dip shit," growled Stein. "If they didn't hear us before, they've fucking heard us now. Go get the rest of the men to bring the boxes here. Fucking schnell!"

Gasping for his breath and totally distressed Scorzeny frantically unloaded the trolley and pushed it back to the men in the relief tunnel just as Sergeant Braun approached, accompanied by Hauptmann Ernst Hoffman wearing overshoes to protect his highly polished jackboots. The men scrambled to their feet as their officer approached and Scorzeny arrived with the empty trolley. Ernst Hoffman noticed Scorzeny's wretched face.

"Scorzeny, you look frightened. Have you seen the enemy in there?"

Corporal Stein emerged from the attack tunnel playing out electric cable.

"We need to hurry. Scorzeny just dropped a box telling the enemy exactly where we are. They could bury us any minute and..."

"Schnell!' shouted Sergeant Braun, "Get the explosives into place. Schnell, schnell.[28] Move now!"

They started immediately loading trolleys with explosives as Ernst Hoffman began his retreat shuffling quietly backwards. Corporal Stein was the first to see this and he gave Sergeant Braun the eye indicating Hoffman's retreat.

"Hauptmann Hoffman," said Braun, "bring the exploder and detonation cord from the pile behind you. Schnell, before we are buried here."

The colour drained from Hoffman's face and everyone stopped what they were doing to look at him. The moment was exquisite for Stein and Scorzeny - their faces beamed sardonically. Literally shitting himself Hoffman turned and quickened his retreating pace. The men hurled lumps of clay after him and, with his face revealing a mix of fear and anger he ran and stumbled headlong into a loaded trolley knocking him out. Corporal Stein looked on as the men dashed forward and picked Hoffman up, placed him on a trolley, wheeled it into the attack tunnel and lay him next to the wall of explosives where they gagged and tied him. Stein smiled knowingly as the men continued to stack the explosives around and over Hoffman entombing him with an explosive coffin.

"I am so glad I am Bavarian or maybe I would be part of his disappearing act," said Stein.

Braun slapped his shoulder and whispered.

"My men have been with me for years. We're all from the same colliery back home. Loyalty to each other means more than the

---

[28] schnell - German word meaning quick

Kaiser or any Prussian bastard. We have more respect for our enemy than these prancing fuckers dressed like fucking peacocks."

Stein gulped as he regretted manhandling Scorzeny. He watched him building the stack of explosives neatly around the head and shoulders of Ernst Hoffman and thought, oh fuck, I need to apologise sooner rather than later.

In the West Wing compound Solly gave Kinney a sack of grenades and whispered.

"Johnny said ye are to relieve Andy but maybe ye should stay wi' 'im for a couple of minutes. We're all ready to blow 'ere."

"Aye," said Kinney, "we'll hae a ciggy afore he gans back here. An' dinnae ye forget me if ye blow afore me."

"Fuck off, ye daft bat. I'll come for ye later, now go an' kill some fuckin' Bosch."

Kinney grabbed the sack of grenades and headed for the West Wing tunnel. Bent double he crept along until he had to drop on all fours to reach the breach. He stopped to clear a roof fall and fitted a sett to prevent further falls, which enhanced his already accelerating trepidation - a roof collapse does wonders for your claustrophobia, especially if crawling further in rather than out. He continued his terrible journey to the breach and climbed down into the German underground gallery where Andy sat puffing on a ciggy as he looked through the observation gap to where the Germans would come.

Sensing movement behind him he turned to see Kinney creeping up on him.

"There's something goin' on in t' dark along there. I could hear whisperin' an' maybe a footfall," Andy whispered.

Both of them stood still with cocked ears listening. Silence.

"Och, ye've been 'ere too long on your own man. Ye should... Feck!"

A smoking grenade rolled between his legs, dropped from a hand through the observation gap. Quick as lightning Kinney picked it up and threw it back through the gap where it exploded twenty yards away - then silence as the two Scots eyeballed each other momentarily.

Kinney grabbed a sandbag and stuffed it in the gap leaving just enough room to peep through. Looking through the hole he saw a figure emerge from the smoke holding another grenade and tried to push it through the peephole, all the time screaming and pushing. Blocking the hole with his fist Kinney removed it momentarily to fire his pistol, blowing the mad face away and the grenade exploded harmlessly just a second later. He looked at Andy and snarled.

"If they are all like him, we'se fecked cos ye didnae see 'im comin' an' nay did I. Feckin' light yon feckin' fuse the noo!"

Again Kinney looked through the peep hole and saw a muzzle flash then blackness as the sniper's bullet crashed through his eye, dragging his brains out of the back of his head. Keeping his cool Andy struck the fuse match and pressed it into the core of the safety fuse igniting it with a hiss. For just a moment he knelt and muttered.

"Och, I'll sing ta ye in the glen auld Highland warrior. The Brave."

With tears in his eyes he ran like hell to the breach and climbed up into the West Wing tunnel where he crawled along on all fours in the darkness toward the light ahead of him where he could stand up. His eyes glittered with fear and hope as the blast fired him along the tunnel like a dart from a blowpipe at one hundred miles per hour straight into the solid wall, which collapsed and buried him forever along with the remains of his pal Kinney.

The explosion shook the vast West Wing compound. Dust fell from the timbered roof and debris and smoke billowed out of the West Wing tunnel entrance blocking it with rubble. At the far end of the compound the sappers crouched around the entrance to the communication tunnel, all looking at each other questioningly as Johnny appeared in the entrance, his face dark with dirt and anger.

"Solly, come wi' me," said Johnny, turning to the others, "Connect yon fuckin' shot blaster ready t' blow."

Scrambling to his feet he ran with Solly to the West Wing tunnel but saw they could go no further. It was blocked.

147

"They didn't make it, Staff," Solly whispered.

"They did, they just got to hell afore us."

"An' here's me thinkin' I'm already in hell," said Solly. "Fuckin' 'ell Staff, you've gotta find safer jobs for us. We've lost four men in as many days an' here's ye wi' a new son."

That stung Johnny. He grabbed Solly's webbing and yanked him down nose to nose.

"Do not lay that fuckin' shit on me or I'll shoot thee my fuckin' self."

Solly struggled free and backed off defensively, stuttering.

"I didn't mean any harm, Staff. Don't send me to another squad. What's left of my life is here wi' thee an' my pals."

Johnny shrugged off his anger and his eyes saddened as he mourned the loss of Andy and Kinney.

"First, Billy Nolan, then Taff and now Andy an' Kinney. I don't want t' lose any more men, especially thee, ye big lug. I need a sergeant, a corporal and more men an' I reckon ye 'ave earned yer corporal's stripes. C'mon, let's kill some fuckin' Bosch," he muttered.

Silently, they made their way back to the sappers who were casually smoking and drinking tea with Jim Connor.

"I've got a pan of all-in stew on t' stove wi' some fresh bread. Would ye like some now, or after t' blow?" he said.

Johnny looked at his men, each face in turn.

"Are they still makin' a noise down there?"

"If anything, they are workin' harder since that blast. Where's Kinney an' Andy?" asked Allballs.

The sadness in Johnny's eyes wiped the smile off Jim Connor's face.

"They didn't make it, the two bangs we 'eard could have been grenades but the third was definitely a rifle shot. But for sure t' fuse was lit an' we'll never know what acts of valour took place in that hole," said Johnny.

"It maybe not right time t' say this but new men are back at rear echelon," said Jim Connor. "Ye should go an' look 'em over. I hear one of 'em is from Bold Colliery, a big lad, Albert Jennings I think. Blow yer hole now an' fuck off. This war waits fer no fucker."

Silently Johnny grabbed a stethoscope and crawled down the communication tunnel on all fours. Reaching the sandbag tamping he checked the safety fuse and electric cables and started using the stethoscope, placing it to the roof, listening intently, feeling the enemy was so close he could smell them.

Allballs crept down to him and whispered for Johnny to get out.

"Hellfire Jack wants thee up top."

They crawled back to the exit and half in half out Johnny looked up at Hellfire Jack.

"What's up, sir?" asked Johnny.

"According to my plans, I reckon Jerry has got his sums wrong. You are directly under his mine. Yes?"

Johnny nodded affirmatively.

"Well, you are about forty yards that away," he pointed west, back down the tunnel. "So, to hurt our galleries he needs to be at least thirty-five yards nearer. So you can blow him now and we'll all go for some breakfast. What!"

He realised his cheerful demeanour was lost on these men.

"Staff Sergeant Gordon, have you got something to tell me?"

Johnny stood up and dusted himself down as the others stood to attention. Hellfire Jack was totally bemused as Johnny spoke.

"The breach in t' West Wing took two o' my men an' I can only assume they're dead because most of the gallery has collapsed an' will take days t' repair it."

Hellfire Jack harrumphed and pondered awhile then whispered.

"Right. Bloody hell. Right blow this mine and take your men back to rear HQ and make the most of a rest and hot food. Five new men will report to you before your next shift, tomorrow night. Yes?"

"Very good, sir," said Johnny, "but will my men receive gallantry awards for dying t' way they did? Their families deserve something for their sacrifice."

"During the last ten days," said Hellfire Jack, "hundreds of thousands of men have been killed in action on this front. I hope their families will get more than a gong and a bit of ribbon. Give their names to the Regimental Chief Clerk, as though he hasn't got enough to do. Damned bloody cheek. I didn't expect that from you."

"Just one more thing, sir," said Johnny.

"What?"

"I need a corporal an' I thought thee might promote one o' my men, sir."

Piqued, Hellfire Jack stage whispered with a snarl.

"I just informed you, five new men will report to you tomorrow night. One of them will be a corporal, and Captain Hamilton-Fox is your new squadron commander. Report to him when you finish here. Carry on."

Hellfire Jack strode away to climb the Requiem shaft ladder to fresh air.

"He talks to me like that at least twice a week," said Jim Connor. "He needs some sleep I don't know how the fuck he does it. He's all over this front line, in an' out of dozens of tunnels. Don't fret, thee'll get what thee wants and he won't mention it again."

"Bully fer 'im," said Johnny, "but 'e doesn't do what we do," he turned to Allballs. "Get back down t' hole wi' t' stethoscope an' tell me when they stop makin' a noise. We'll eat now and Yiggs'll relieve ye shortly."

Allballs crawled down the hole as the others headed for Jim Connor's shed to get some food in their bellies.

In the German relief tunnel, Sergeant Braun lit a ciggie and offered one to Corporal Stein, who took it and lit it off the same match. Private Scorzeny and the others were taking the last of the explosives into the attack tunnel and stacking the boxes to the roof. Scorzeny dropped to his knees and whispered into a tiny gap between the boxes.

"I hope you can hear me, you pompous Prussian bastard. You are about to go to Hell in the tiniest of pieces. Open your eyes, you cowardly turd. I want you to be awake to start your journey. I wish I could undo the gag so I can hear your screams."

The poor light of the tunnel was just enough to see one eye opened - that was how Scorzeny had built the boxes around Hoffman's head. He had waited a long time for this.

"Ha, you are awake. It is I, Scorzeny, the Bavarian, the one who is in that grey area. Remember? Along with three soldiers you were going to execute for cowardice in the face of the enemy. How ironic for you to be waiting your turn to die for being a coward."

Sergeant Braun and Corporal Stein joined him at the pile of explosives.

"On your feet, Scorzy," said Braun, "we're going to detonate now. Wish him bon voyage and fuck off."

Scorzeny muttered something to Hoffman and scurried away as Stein connected the cable to the detonator.

Not so far away in Jim Connor's shed were the sappers eating his all-in stew and in better spirits, although sorrow was still in the air around them.

"Sithee, Staff, shall I go an' relieve Allballs?" Yiggs asked.

With his mouth full of stew Johnny nodded approval and Yiggs scampered away to the communication tunnel and crawled down to Allballs.

"I can hear three men up there, an' possibly six or seven men a few yards back. One of them just said auf wiedersehen so they must be finished an' ready t' blow. There's nowt else, so we need t' blow. C'mon, fuck off."

The two sappers quickly crawled out to see Johnny standing there waiting for them. He was holding the shot blaster and ready to hit the T plunger.

"Are they all still there?" he asked.

"They've stopped working but they are still there, ready t' blow. Fire it now an' we've got 'em," said Allballs.

Very quickly they filled the tunnel entrance with sandbags and stepped back as Johnny grabbed the plunger.

In the German relief tunnel the men loaded their tools and equipment onto a trolley and started filling the attack tunnel entrance with sandbags. Corporal Stein was uncoiling electric cable as he slowly moved along the tunnel. A shot blaster was attached to a webbing strap slung over his shoulder as Sergeant Braun supervised his men blocking the attack tunnel entrance.

He heard footfalls and voices approaching. He saw Corporal Stein stand to attention as a group of officers surrounded him. Stein pointed to Sergeant Braun. The group of officers approached Sergeant Braun and one of them beckoned him. He marched to meet them and stood to attention.

"Where is Hauptmann Hoffman?" the officer asked.

"Safe in his bunker, I imagine," replied Braun.

"I detect a hint of sourness, Sergeant. You are Bavarian, yes?"

"We all are here at the sharp end. Not really the place to see officers such as your good selves," said Braun.

"Your remarks are borderline insolence, Sergeant. Perhaps a day or two in the trenches will curb your tongue."

"If you don't mind, sir," said Braun, "we need to move further along the tunnel so we can fire our mine."

"Where is the mine?" the officer asked.

Sergeant Braun pointed to his men.

"My men are blocking the entrance to prevent back blast, a necessary task for all our mines."

"Show me," ordered the officer.

"The entrance is just there, sir. There's nothing to see."

"Show me the mine, Sergeant."

"But sir, that means…"

"Show me the fucking mine!"

Overhearing this, Stein quickly placed the cable and shot blaster on the ground and sneaked away into the darkness. The men dismantled the sandbag wall in the entrance to the attack tunnel and sergeant Braun handed the officer a torch as he squatted to squirm through without going on all fours. The other officers lined up to follow - all this just to save face.

In his explosive coffin Ernst Hoffman could see nothing but heard everything. His chance of staying alive came closer as the group were able to stand in the small cavern of explosives.

"Silence! What is that humming noise? Call the sergeant in here."

The officer shushed everyone to silence as Hoffman hummed frantically through his nose. An officer bent down and shouted along the tunnel.

"Sergeant! Get in here now."

Knowing his enemy would have heard the shouting, Sergeant Braun gathered his men.

"They have found Hoffman. Connect the blaster and fire it. Don't wait for me. Go now."

Dumbfounded the men stood there awkwardly but when Scorzeny ran toward the blaster, they soon caught up with him.

In the silence of the West Wing compound Johnny heard the Germans shouting and whispered to Yiggs and Allballs.

"They must think they're fuckin' fireproof. Quick, get everyone up the Requiem shaft out of harms way. We're about ninety feet deep 'ere an' their bomb isn't going to blow upwards to make a crater. It'll follow the path of least resistance an' possibly blast through 'ere. Go now. Fuck off."

The two sappers sprinted to Jim Connor's shed and Johnny watched them all racing for the Requiem shaft ladder. Stepping to the side of the entrance he looked down to see the electric cable buried beneath the sandbags. He hit the plunger. Nothing. He pulled back the plunger and hit it again. Nothing. Frantically he pulled away the sandbags that blocked the entrance and crawled along all the way down to the sandbag wall, behind which were the torpedoes. Madly searching for the fuse matches he delved into his bullet pouch and pulled out a box of matches and with it the little robin, which tweeted loudly as it dropped to the ground.

"Bloody 'ell! It's thee again."

He swiftly scooped up the bedraggled robin, put it back in the bullet pouch and hurriedly struck a match, pushing it into the scarfed[29] end of the safety fuse.

"Great Lord of the universe, please help me now."

The match fizzled out. In frenzy he lit another. That is when he heard a baby cry.

"Oh, sweet Jesus!"

He forced the match into the core of the safety fuse. A fizz and off it burned, sparkling through the tiny gap in the sandbag wall. He checked his watch and crawled like hell toward the exit.

The robin tweeted.

In the German relief tunnel, Private Scorzeny connected the cable to the brass segments on the blaster and without looking hit the plunger. An enormous explosion obliterated the attack tunnel, vaporising everything to create a gigantic cavern and ball of fire that ripped through the gallery incinerating everything and everyone. Corporal Stein felt a shock wave in the air of the tunnel and smirked knowingly as he heard the explosion. He picked out a ciggie and, in a split second of vision, saw it disintegrate along with his hand as he instantly turned to ash.

Approaching the compound at the end of the communication tunnel, Johnny felt the earth beneath him tremble.

"Fuckin' 'ell!"

He crawled faster but was buried by the falling roof just as he arrived at the compound. Timbers pinned him down as tons of earth tumbled down on top of him trapping his legs. The entrance to the communication tunnel was hidden beneath tons of earth as the deep

---

[29] scarf - join the ends of two pieces of timber or metal by bevelling or notching them so they fit over or into each other

roaring noise diminished to that of creaking timbers. Eventually silence.

Then voices were calling from a long way away, ninety feet up the ladder at the top of the Requiem shaft. The sappers each carrying spades, scrambled down the ladder ignoring Jim Connor's pleas for safety. Other sappers now appeared and set about rerigging the winch and overhead pulley that lifted sandbags and loaded trolleys to the surface. Miners' rescue teams worked to a frenzied pace to save their comrades and these men were in full swing working like clockwork.

Johnny's men had reached the bottom of Requiem shaft and were appalled at the sight of the caved in tunnel. Nevertheless they started digging as more men arrived with spades and sandbags. Nobody spoke as they dug like hell and the spoil was hoisted up to the surface. Furiously digging, one man stopped.

"Sithee, how many men are trapped down here?" he asked.

"One," came the reply.

"One! Who is it?"

"Staff Sergeant Johnny Gordon," came back the chorus.

"Shut up and dig," somebody shouted.

Underneath the rubble Johnny was fast slipping away and struggling to breathe. In a dream-like state he heard voices like that of his men, mingled with the voice of his wife and the cooing of a baby. He heard a voice, 'ye reap what ye sow, sergeant'. Lying trapped in a near foetal position, able only to move the fingers of one hand, he tried to reach his face but could not. He tried to speak but no. 'Great Holy Father, shine your light on the son I will not see. I beseech thee never to let him witness that which I have seen', and then he passed into unconsciousness as he accidentally flicked open his bullet pouch. The bedraggled little robin's head popped out.

"Tweet!"

Allballs had heard something.

"Hush! Quiet, fuckin' shut up. Listen, I just heard a bird, down there, listen."

The silence was strangely expectant.

"Tweet!"

"Sithee! Dig straight down there."

As they dug more earth collapsed. So wooden setts were inserted to hold back falling soil. They dug furiously, sweating and cursing French soil. A dirty hand was exposed and a cheer went up from the men. Tools were dropped and the men dug with their bare hands. Solly cleared muck from around the wrist then felt for a pulse.

"Nothing. Aww fuckin' hell! Wait, I just felt a tiny throb. Yes, it's very weak, fuckin' get him out!"

Solly frantically cleared muck from around the arm as he tried to expose the face. Tat scrambled out of the hole and yelled.

"Get the Oxygen Resuscitation Kit an' a stretcher down 'ere now. An' have a medic standing by up there."

Allballs and Solly cleared the muck from around the head and Solly gently removed the helmet. The other miners expertly removed earth from around the timbers that trapped the legs. They could see the timbers had broken both legs and the tibia and femur bones protruded grotesquely from each. Solly opened Johnny's mouth and plucked out the debris, clearing the airways.

"C'mon, Johnny, this is no time for malingering. Hellfire Jack'll have our guts for garters if we don't wake ye up."

"Don't wake him 'til we get him on t' stretcher," said Tat. "He'll be in too much fuckin' pain when we move him."

Allballs pulled the stretcher into place and the men gently lifted Johnny onto it, his broken limbs dangling uselessly. Brummie fitted the resuscitation kit on the stretcher and placed the oxygen mask over Johnny's mouth.

"All set," he shouted. "Hoist away carefully."

The stretcher was too long to fit horizontally in the tubular steel shaft so it had to ascend at an angle with Brummie climbing the ladder at the head end and Solly beneath him at the foot end. At the top two miners turned the winch handles as Brummie climbed out of the shaft carefully holding the oxygen mask to Johnny's face.

Clearing the rim of the shaft Solly appeared holding the stretcher steady as the winch men lowered it to the ground.

A medical orderly crouched over Johnny and quickly assessed the visible injuries, negatively shaking his head.

"His pelvis is fair smashed and his spine is likely broken, ooh arr," he said, with a Devonian accent.

"Don't write him off yet, ye fuckin' scrumpy head," said Yiggs.

"Us west country boys knows our way around broken bodies better 'n any fuckin' grockle, so shut yer fuckin' yap 'n gerrim o'er to the casualty tents wi 'out gerrin shot. Sniper are busy at dawn."

Solly and Brummie each grabbed a handle at the head end while Tat and Yiggs got the foot end of the stretcher, as Allballs held back the tarp so they could exit. Allballs then ran to the outer tarp so they could meet the fresh air of the French dawn and the ravaged landscape of trenches and shell craters.

Across the battlefield, motionless in his hide, the German sniper waited patiently for his moment. Slowly he brought the crosshairs in his telescopic sight to line up on the tallest head and - crack! The bullet entered the side of the face and took off half of the skull and all of the brains as Solly fell.

*

That was the moment Beryl experienced the most intense orgasm in her life and her love for Cathryn nearly burst her heart. Between passionate kisses and caresses she murmured.

"Just a wee while ago ye came on my tongue and whispered that thee will love me forevermore. Well for some reason I feel the same for thee and our lives will be blessed from this moment on."

She reached across to the bedside table and turned the smiling photo of Solly face down. Something inside her made her think she would never see him again. That fleeting moment of sadness departed the moment Cathryn's lips kissed each of her breasts.

*

157

Solly lay in the blood and muck of the trench looking skywards with open sightless eyes. Brummie knelt and closed them and uttered.

"Fuck," looking along the trench he uttered, "fuck," again, as a fresh young face and clean uniform stumbled into view. Albert Jennings had arrived.

Young Albert did not know he had been mentioned in dispatches. Not in the military sense but in the letters from wives to husbands in the trenches and tunnels on the Western Front.

"I hear thee's got a piss pot scar on t' head," Brummie said as the sappers picked up the stretcher.

The urge to shit once again liquefied Albert's guts and he gladly rushed forward.

"Just take a quick peek over t' fire step, see if all's clear for us," Brummie said.

The crosshairs lined up and - crack! Right between the eyes and Albert joined Solly, minus the back of his head. Brummie smirked uncontrollably and felt a pang of elation as he bowed his head so the sniper would not see him. The others also stooped low and heard Brummie mutter.

"Danke, Herr Scharfschütze[30]."

Grim smiles cracked the dried clay on the faces of the stretcher-bearers revealing, only to themselves, that the continuous existence of life and death on the battlefield had turned the once normal, hardworking and proud men of the north into semi-savage warriors up against the stark realities of survival. Incidents such as what happened to Albert Jennings and Captain Davidson would haunt the memories of those who survived this terrible war.

In the poor light of dawn, the sappers trudged and stumbled through trenches where groups of men huddled around camping stoves brewing tea and cooking breakfast. The sappers stoically carried Johnny to the rear echelon Casualty Clearing Area where the

---

[30] Danke, Herr Scharfschütze – thank you Mr Sniper

dead lay in rows as far as the eye could see. Setting the stretcher down amongst hundreds of wounded men the sappers looked around for a medic. Brummie and Allballs could not believe their eyes when they saw a blood-spattered nurse wearing a nosebag like a papoose on her back as she tended to the wounded.

"Sithee, yonder nurse still has our baby. Holy Mother of God, look!" said Allballs.

Puzzled, Yiggs looked to see what all the fuss was about.

"We need to find a medic smartish if we're to save Johnny. Whassup?" he said.

"We've found our own Florence Nightingale. Look, she still has the baby Johnny saved the other day," said Brummie.

Allballs approached the nurse who looked up at him. Immediately recognising him she stood up and gave the most beautiful smile. He pointed to Johnny.

"Remember I told ye about Johnny saving t' baby? He's o'er yonder on t' stretcher badly wounded because a tunnel roof caved in on him."

Holding her by the hand he took her over to Johnny. The four sappers and the nurse knelt by Johnny as she unhitched the nosebag and lifted out the baby, who instantly awoke making baby noises like they do.

The warriors were enchanted by the baby and so was Johnny. The baby looked at Johnny and they all saw he was awake. In this extraordinary moment the moaning of the wounded and the sounds of battle ceased as the baby and Johnny smiled at each other. One last glance at each of his men, as their tears cut through the clay on their faces and they watched his eyes glaze over at the departure of his soul.

As Johnny's eyes closed his journey to the angels began and the little robin popped out and joined him flying high over the fields of France.

THE END

A British soldier, John J. Gordon, died of his wounds at Trones Wood during the Battle of the Somme on 11th July 1916. He is buried in Etaples cemetery in France.

R.I.P. Johnny

ABOUT THE AUTHOR

Christopher Chance was born in Widnes and was educated at St Bede's School, St John Fisher and St Thomas More School.

He was further educated in the Corps of Royal Engineers where he served twelve years as a Combat Engineer Class 1. During his twelve years in the military he worked in Engineer Intelligence with the British Army on the Rhine (BAOR) and as an Intelligence Operator in Northern Ireland. He was an Anti-interrogation instructor, a Small Arms School Corps weapons instructor, and an explosives and demolitions expert.

On leaving the armed forces he entered the Licensed Trade and became a restaurateur, a member of the Guild of Sommeliers and a member of the British Institute of Innkeepers. After several years as a restaurateur he left England to set up his martial arts business with his wife in Spain, where they opened two schools of martial arts on the Costa del Sol.

His interest in the martial arts started many years ago when he trained at the Singapore Karate Club in 1965 and this grew throughout his military career and throughout his adult life. He holds dan grades (Black Belt) in ju-jitsu and karate and was the international representative for the World Combat Federation in Spain and Portugal. His circle of friends includes many top martial artists around the world.

Christopher now dedicates his time to writing and healthy living.

161

Also by the author

The Lone Brit on 13 - ISBN1-84018- 957-6
Carabanchel - ISBN 1-84018-967-3
The Assassins Code 1 - ISBN 9781907340123
Satan's Arena - eBook only

Use the link below to see his printed books available from his
website and various outlets.

www.chrischance.co.uk

AVAILABLE FROM
STRAND PUBLISHING UK LTD

Ingram Content Group UK Ltd.
Milton Keynes UK
UKHW040724080323
418175UK00004B/453

9 781907 340253